5x19(18)

DATE DUE

BRODART, CO.   Cat. No. 23-221

MINRS3

ALSO BY
KEVIN SYLVESTER

MiNRS

MiNRS 2

THE MINRS SERIES CONTINUES IN

MINRS3

KEVIN SYLVESTER

SIMON &
SCHUSTER
CANADA

New York London Toronto Sydney New Delhi

SIMON & SCHUSTER CANADA

A Division of Simon & Schuster, Inc.

166 King Street East, Suite 300

Toronto, Ontario M5A 1J3

This book is a work of fiction. Any references to historical events, real people, or real places are used fictitiously. Other names, characters, places, and events are products of the author's imagination, and any resemblance to actual events or places or persons, living or dead, is entirely coincidental.

Text copyright © 2018 by Kevin Sylvester

For information about special discounts for bulk purchases, please contact Simon & Schuster Special Sales at 1-800-268-3216 or CustomerService@simonandschuster.ca.

Book design by Sonia Chaghatzbanian

The text for this book was set in ITC Garamond Std.

Manufactured in the United States of America

0418 FFG

First Edition

10 9 8 7 6 5 4 3 2 1

Library and Archives Canada Cataloguing in Publication

Sylvester, Kevin, author

 Minrs 3 / Kevin Sylvester.

Issued in print and electronic formats.

ISBN 978-1-5011-9528-0 (hardcover).—ISBN 978-1-5011-9530-3 (ebook)

I. Title. II. Title: Minrs three.

PS8637.Y42M56 2018   jC813'.6   C2018-901028-2   C2018-901029-0

**To the types of people
who read the acknowledgments**

Chapter One
Stupid

"This plan is stupid." Pavel loomed over me, his shadow spreading across the map I'd just unfurled on top of a rock. The rest of the group was cleaning up after our makeshift dinner—canned beans and canned beans—but somehow Pavel had weaseled his way out of helping.

"I haven't even started explaining it yet," I said, placing stones on the edges to hold them down.

"Okay. I'm sure this plan is *going* to be stupid."

"Feel free to stay behind," I said, not looking up. Pavel didn't respond. He also didn't move, so his shadow stayed right where I didn't want it.

Boots scrunched on pebbles as the rest of the group began to make their way over.

I slid the map noisily into the sunlight and readjusted the stones. I pulled my battered notebook out of my pocket and checked my calculations one more time.

Then I carefully drew an arc around a large circle on the far right of the paper.

"What's that for?" Elena asked, leaning in next to me for a closer look. Her hand rested on mine for a second and she gave an almost imperceptible squeeze.

I finished the line and leaned back. "A trajectory. This is the only path we can take if we have any hope of reaching Earth. The big circle is Perses." I pointed with my pencil, then traced along the arc, ending at a smaller circle I'd drawn in the upper left. "This is Earth. It's clearly not to scale," I joked. No one laughed.

Elena chewed meditatively on her lower lip. I watched her, remembering the first time I'd seen her do that, on the ship that brought us here from Earth. "But you drew the line *around* Perses."

"If we try to head to Earth on a *straight* line we'll run out of energy. And if we run out of that . . ." I let the rest hang in the air.

Out of the corner of my eye, I caught Darcy squirming. She was sitting on the ground a few feet away, pretending not to listen. She was clearly listening intently. My shoulders sagged. Darcy had just turned six. Six.

Way too young to see what she'd seen, live through what we'd all lived through.

"But won't we burn more fuel going *around* Perses?" Fatima's voice pulled me back from my thoughts.

Therese stood next to her looking down at the map, frowning. "Fatima's right. I mean, you've made it a longer trip, right?"

"Technically, yes. In distance but not in time." That was met with more blank stares. "The transport ship isn't designed to travel quickly, or to go a long way. Certainly not all the way back to Earth."

"Isn't that a reason to take the *shortest* route?" Fatima asked.

I closed my eyes and rubbed my forehead. "Look, I know I'm not explaining this well."

"No kidding," Elena said with a chuckle.

"We need to build up enough momentum and speed to get us there. This way, we'll actually burn *less* fuel than we would on a direct path."

"By traveling farther?" Therese said. "I still don't get it."

"Yes, it's a little risky, but the math works," I said.

"A little risky," Elena repeated.

"And we're flying a ship, not an equation," Fatima said.

"Is there anything that's just a *little* risky in space?" Mandeep asked.

"No," I admitted, my face reddening. "Not really."

"Stupid," Pavel muttered. He turned and walked away, shaking his head.

I watched him go, then looked at Elena and rolled my eyes.

Elena frowned. "Yeah, he's a pain. But is he wrong?"

"It's not stupid. It is risky. Like I said, the math makes sense. You use the gravitational pull of a planet to add speed to your trajectory. You kind of piggyback on the force of the larger object. Look." I started writing out the formula next to the line.

Elena arched her eyebrow, our standard "you're geeking out" signal, and I stopped writing. "Just stick to the quick version," she said.

Mandeep snapped her fingers, the sound so sudden and loud that I jumped. "Wait. We studied this in school, right?"

"Yeah," I said, catching my breath.

"Gravity something? Your mom was talking about it just before the . . ." It had been one of her last science lessons before our colony was attacked and all our parents were killed. It seemed like years ago. But it still felt raw.

"Gravity assist," I said. "They do this with satellites all the time."

"Oh yeah," Elena said. "Your mom said they used the gravity of the moon for some slingshot thing. This is that?"

I nodded. "It's sometimes called the slingshot effect."

Elena looked up at the sky. The sun, slightly larger than it appeared on Earth, blazed away. "I don't see any moon up there, Chris."

Elena had hit on the biggest question mark in this whole plan. She had a knack for that.

"True," I said. "But I think there is a different way to do the same thing, using Perses itself."

"You *think*?"

I sighed and held my left arm up, cocked at the elbow, my hand pointing toward the sky. "Say this is our ship." I made a sound like a blasting rocket and lifted my arm and hand higher. "We break out of the atmosphere, which is what this ship is designed to do." I pointed at my hand. "But then we stop, turn, and fall back toward Perses." I swooped my hand in a semicircle down toward the ground.

"And we crash," Fatima said. "Boom." She mimicked a mushroom cloud with her hands.

"No, we don't. We get pulled back by the gravity of Perses, but as we fall we pick up speed. Then we accelerate on an angle that lets us break free of the pull at the right moment, with more force than when we began. We whip around the planet," I swooped my hand back up faster, "and get shot out toward Earth."

I didn't add that my calculations needed to be exact or else we *would* get pulled right back down . . . or else shot off in an entirely wrong direction. "It's not the most scientific explanation, but do you all get it?" Everyone was staring intently at my hand.

"What?"

Elena pointed up.

I looked. A trickle of blood had begun to run down from the knuckles between my remaining fingers. I'd injured the wound during our battle with Thatcher's troops, while scratching my way down a tunnel to plant the powerful bomb that had secured our victory. The battle itself had only ended a few days before. There had been no time to rest, or heal. Everyone was nursing some injury or other.

I pulled my hand down and jammed it in my armpit to stem the bleeding, cursing—more out of embarrassment than worry or pain.

"I hope the ship is sturdier than your hand," Fatima said with a snort.

"Ha ha," I said, pulling my hand out. The flow of blood had at least slowed down.

Mandeep took a quick look. "I'll go get my medical kit and close the stitches up. Again." She walked back to the transport.

Elena pulled a rag from her pants pocket and handed it to me.

"Sorry," I said, wrapping it tightly around my hand.

"No need to apologize, Fearless Leader. Just making sure it doesn't get infected."

"Too much force breaking your hand out of orbit?" Fatima said.

"A ship is slightly better built than my stupid hand," I said, squeezing the rag hard.

"But you think this plan will actually work?" Elena said. Her voice didn't have the hard edge I was used to. She was worried. I stole another look at Darcy, who was sitting still but with an ear cocked in our direction.

"Yes," I said, as confidently as I could. Then I leaned closer to Elena and Fatima and whispered, "But we will have to exit the gravity pull at the exact correct angle or the ship could fly in a completely different direction. Then we'd waste even more fuel trying to get back on track."

"We could turn around and come back here," Fatima said. "Try again later."

I stared at her without saying anything.

"Oh," she whispered. "This is a one-way trip?"

I nodded. "One way or another. One full gas tank. One chance to escape."

Elena and Fatima looked at each other without talking. I was struck by how close we'd all become in the last few weeks. Elena and Fatima were, to me, a perfect example of how grinders and miners could work together. And I was also struck by how much I needed them to agree with me, and to support me.

I noticed my own hands clenching as I waited for their answer.

They nodded at each other and looked back at me.

"We're still in." My fists relaxed.

"STUPID," Pavel called from somewhere behind the transport.

Chapter Two
Flight

One of the perks of opening the transport had been the discovery of clean pillows, blankets, and sheets. We'd salvaged some mattresses from the wreckage of the nearby core-scraper and made our new "home" pretty comfortable.

It was surprisingly big. We seemed to keep discovering nooks and crannies and rooms, including a large cargo hold, which was good because it meant we didn't need to sleep in the same room all the time.

Not that I was sleeping much. We planned to leave in two days, and I just couldn't stop running and rerunning the calculations in my mind. There were a dozen things that had to go right, and a million that could easily go wrong.

The calculations in my notebook didn't cheer me up.

> **V = our velocity approaching Perses**
>
> **U = the velocity of Perses**
>
> **V2 (2U + V) = our exit speed, after gaining energy from Perses**
>
> **96 degrees — the successful angle of exit**
>
> **100 degrees — we'd end up on Pluto, if we were lucky**
>
> **92 degrees — we'd crash on Perses, going too fast to slow down**

I tweaked the value for *V* over and over and over.

The numbers danced in front of my eyes. *V* equals 90 kilometers per second? Then *V2* would be more like 180 kilometers per second. That would get us back to Earth in about a month, but would the ship handle the force? That was something I just couldn't know until we tried it.

We could play it safer, but then would we survive the trip?

> **80km/s? Two months**
>
> **70? Three**

Analyzing numbers can be like counting sheep and finally, exhausted, I fell asleep. That didn't stop the numbers from dancing in my mind. It also didn't keep away the nightmare images of our spaceship hurtling toward the stars or crashing back to the surface of Perses.

In the end, it wasn't a restful sleep, or a very long one.

"DARCY!"

I woke with a start as Therese's voice split the air of the cabin.

"Darcy!" She called, over and over.

I sat up straight and threw off my blankets. I could hear the others doing the same. A cool damp bit at my toes. The door was wide open. I could see stars twinkling in the distance and then Therese's shadow blocking the dim light. She fumbled with her helmet and flicked on the headlamp.

"Therese, what is it?" I called. I had to shield my eyes as she turned toward me.

"Darcy is gone." She spun around and rushed out the door.

I jammed my feet in my boots, not bothering to tie them, and grabbed my helmet. The room was soon filled with light as everyone rushed to search.

I burst through the doorway. Therese's calls of

"Darcy" grew fainter as her light bobbed up and down frantically on the ground to the east.

I looked down. There were dozens of footprints in the soft, dusty soil, heading in all directions. There was no way to tell where Darcy had gone.

"Everybody fan out," I said.

"I'll go west," Elena said.

"She can't have gone far," Fatima said. "I'll go that way." She pointed north and was off like a shot.

"I'll look around here, then head south," I said. I peeked under the transport. She wasn't there. We'd slid a piece of metal over the hole Elena had discovered under the hull. It was still in place. Good.

"Maybe Pavel saw her," Fatima called to me as she ran off calling Darcy's name.

"Pavel," I said, looking around for any sign of him. I'd totally forgotten he was on guard duty. Had he gone after her? In which direction?

As if on cue, he emerged from behind the transport, strolling toward me slowly, his headlamp lighting up his front as he looked down to do up his zipper.

"Did you see her?" I said, rushing toward him.

"See who?" he said.

He hadn't seen anything. He hadn't been doing his job. "You idiot!"

"What?" he said, looking up suddenly. The headlamp blazed in my eyes, blinding me. At that precise moment I tripped on my untied laces, and I stumbled and plowed into him, knocking him back on the ground. "OW!" he yelled.

We fell to the ground together, and he began punching. I tried to stand up, but he grabbed my shoulder with one hand, then started hitting me with the other.

I swung my arms in front of me to protect myself, but he was able to land a few punches on my nose and cheeks. I punched back, just to get him to stop. We both yelped in pain, and I could feel the blood coming from my nose, lips, and who knew where else.

In desperation, I swung my leg forward and jammed my knee down into his ribs. Winded, he gasped for air and let go of my arm. I stood up and hovered over him.

"You were supposed to be on guard! GUARD! That means keeping an eye on the transport, on everything that happens. Darcy ran away."

He finally began to catch his breath.

"I had to go take a leak!" he said. "I didn't want to wake anybody up using the bathroom, so I just went over there." He pointed to a spot in the distance where some scrubby bushes had begun growing up around the rocks.

"But you didn't see Darcy?"

"No. I was literally gone for like a minute." He reached up and wiped at his forehead, then looked at his hand, which was covered in red. "I need to go clean up," he said, scrambling to his feet. "Jerk," he muttered, just loud enough for me to hear.

"We have to go look for her."

"One minute." He grimaced as he held his ribs and began shuffling toward the transport. "Did you ever consider she might actually be hiding inside the ship?" he called back.

The door to the transport opened and then closed behind him.

I tasted blood and took a deep breath. I walked over, and the doors slid open again.

The lights—on nighttime mode—stayed off. But Pavel had put on his helmet and I could see him sitting on his bed, one of Mandeep's first aid kits open on his lap. He grabbed some medical gauze and began wrapping his knuckles.

"Darcy?" I called. There was no answer. I walked inside and turned left onto the bridge. The door opened and I called again. "Darcy?" I craned my neck to listen, but there was nothing but the occasional hum of a computer and the sound of my own breathing. I walked to the console and turned on the lights.

Empty.

I walked back into the bedroom.

"Darn it," Pavel said. He threw the medical box aside. "There's hardly any gauze left. I'll have to use your pillowcase, Nichols."

There were hurried footsteps from outside. Elena bounded up the stairs and practically smacked into me. She stopped abruptly when she saw my face.

"What the heck happened to you?"

"It was mostly an accident," I said, nodding in Pavel's direction.

"Very mature," she said, eyeing Pavel trying to jam some sheets—my sheets, of course—against his nose to stop the bleeding. He also had a cut on his forehead. He was a total mess.

"I guess that explains the blood all over the stairs and the floor," Elena said.

I looked down. There was more than I'd expected. Pavel's nose and my lip had made the place look like a scene from a horror movie.

"Head wounds," Elena said. "They bleed like crazy."

"Did you find Darcy?"

"Not yet. I came back to get my digger. I can cover more ground that way. She must have gotten a bigger head start than we thought."

She glared at Pavel, who continued wrapping gauze around his head.

"Or she's great at hiding," I said.

"I'm heading north. Why don't you grab Mandeep's digger and go south."

I nodded.

Elena shook her head as she stared at Pavel, who was starting to resemble an Egyptian mummy. "Once you're done prettying up, lock the door and then head southeast."

Pavel snorted something that sounded like an agreement.

Elena reached down and grabbed a towel from the foot of somebody's bed and threw it to me. "Let's get moving."

I took one last look at Pavel, who didn't seem in any rush, then swallowed my anger and headed for my digger.

I desperately wanted to be the one to find Darcy, to maybe help patch the rift that had opened between us.

But it was Pavel. Of all people. He didn't even have to look far.

Darcy had run to the graveyard. He found her huddled up on top of the still-loose earth of Maria's grave, shivering against the cold, asleep.

He carried her back down to the transport and then fired a blast into the air to signal the rest of us.

When we got back, Darcy was lying on her bed, awake but not moving. She stared straight up at the ceiling.

Therese ran over to make sure she was okay. Darcy turned away and pulled the blankets over her head.

I approached her bed and leaned down close to her. "Darcy. Why did you run away?" She refused to answer.

Therese lay down next to her and began singing a lullaby. Soon Darcy was back asleep.

"She talked to me on the walk back," Pavel said. I felt a pang of jealousy, but I forced it away. "She said she doesn't want to say goodbye to Maria, Finn, the others."

Mandeep sighed. "She doesn't want to leave Perses."

"Exactly," Pavel said.

I understood. This was the only home Darcy had ever known. The rest of us had some faint memories of Earth. Some of those were happy—of family vacations and backyard barbecues.

All Darcy had heard about Earth was from the Oracle, telling us that there was a war coming. And that we were going to be part of that war. And that the next battle was going to be fought on Earth.

We needed to get back home to show everyone that

Thatcher and his supporters were dangerous, deadly, power hungry, and evil. We needed to fight the fear he'd fostered with the truth. We had a video of Thatcher killing Nazeem. It needed to be seen. We needed to show what had really happened.

We could turn the tide.

If we made it back alive.

But what kind of life was that? Better or worse than staying here on Perses?

I had no choice. I had to go back.

Did Darcy?

Therese came over to me. "I want to stay here with her," she said. "It's not fair to make her go if she doesn't want to."

My head swam. We'd all grown into a team, a kind of family . . . and now a giant crack had just appeared in that image.

I shook my head. "No. We stick together. We need to stick together." I didn't say that I'd made a vow to myself to look after Darcy. To protect her. Didn't that mean keeping her close? Safe? Didn't it?

Therese put a hand on my shoulder. "I was born and raised on a farm. We can make things grow. There's enough water and shelter to stay alive for months, even longer if we have to. I'm a grinder. I'm a survivor."

"And Darcy?"

"Christopher. You know she's a survivor too. But she's seen enough fighting. And do you think there won't be more fighting when you get back to Earth?"

Darcy turned over in her bed, reaching for her stuffed dog, Friendly. He wasn't there. He'd been buried with Maria.

I fought to keep my voice steady. "What do you do if the Landers come back? If Thatcher isn't dead? If he's out there, waiting?"

"We'll have a battle digger," she said. "And you've taught us how to hide. How to fight."

Darcy frowned in her sleep.

Therese turned and looked at her too. Then she said firmly, "We'll be okay. You'll finish this back on Earth. Then send someone to get us. Give her a few months' peace."

I looked around, pleading for someone else to argue against this plan. But Pavel and Fatima and Mandeep were all staring at their feet. Elena looked straight at me, locking her eyes on mine. She gave an almost imperceptible nod.

I paused, doing my best to keep myself together. Then I nodded back.

Chapter Three
M

I had agreed to split us up. It hurt. It scared me. Then Darcy came up with an idea to keep us connected . . . permanently.

We were sitting at our last dinner together, the crimson sunset adding to our sense of melancholy.

It was warm so Elena had torn her uniform off at the waist, her torso only covered in a tank top. Like so many things she did, this had started a trend. That meant everyone's arms were exposed as we sat and munched on our beans.

So we could clearly see the double-*M* tattoos that marked Fatima and Therese as property of Melming Mining. My own father had one, but it was only after his death that I'd discovered it was a brand.

Darcy pointed at Therese's arm, then at Fatima's.

"What is it?" Therese asked.

"Yeah, do I have baked beans on my shirt?" Fatima joked.

Darcy shook her head and without saying a word, she dipped her finger in her beans and used the sauce to draw an *M* on her own arm. Then she pointed at the rest of us.

"What?" Elena asked. "You want a tattoo?" She chuckled.

Darcy nodded her head.

Elena stopped chuckling. "Seriously? Kiddo, I'm not sure. You know . . ."

Darcy crossed her arms, lowered her head, and glared at Elena. She was clearly serious.

"You tell them, Therese," Darcy whispered, her eyes still on Elena. "No one ever listens to me."

Therese shuffled in her seat, clearly a little unsure of what to say. She coughed. "Darcy was thinking that it's unfair that we have these brands while everyone else is 'normal.' Thatcher used that word, right, Chris?"

"Something like that."

Darcy pointed at Therese's arm. "Evil," she said.

"She says we should all have them," Therese said.

Everyone looked from Therese to Darcy.

"I'm game," Elena said, shrugging. She immediately held out her arm. "I've already got enough scars from the Landers, might as well have one I want."

"This is NOT a good idea," Mandeep said.

"I'm not getting some stupid grinder tattoo," Pavel insisted.

"Shut up, Pavel," Darcy said. We all stared at her, shocked. "I want one." Her eyes snapped toward Mandeep. "Now."

Mandeep gaped at her.

"Now!" Darcy repeated.

"Okay then," I said, breaking the awkward silence. "I'm in too. But maybe we make it something a little different."

"What does he mean?" Darcy asked Therese, not looking at me.

"This." I took a pen and drew the Melming Mining logo on a napkin. Then I connected the bigger and the smaller *M*s to make one big *M*. I filled in the space and declared, "*M* for MiNRs," placing the pen back on the table.

"MiNRs," Darcy said. She rolled up her sleeve.

And that settled it.

Mandeep slathered everything with enough

disinfectant to kill an elephant-sized germ. That didn't stop it from hurting when she used a hot needle and some ink on our arms. I had to sacrifice the last of my old-school pens, but I told myself it was for Darcy. Mandeep began with Elena, who actually succeeded in making Darcy giggle by pulling goofy faces each time Mandeep poked her with the needle.

Her resistance to pain was epic.

Pavel still refused. "I'm not a grinder," he grumbled.

I yanked him outside while Fatima was getting her tattoo "fixed."

"What is your deal?" I said.

"Seriously? Why would anyone want to get a hot needle poked in their arm?"

"I'm not thrilled. But it's for Darcy, and I think it means a lot to her."

Pavel rolled his eyes.

"And it's a good idea. Those brands single Fatima and Therese out."

"And you don't think people can tell a grinder from a real human anyway?" He made a sniffing sound, like he'd detected a bad smell.

"I thought you'd gotten over that crap." I clenched my fists. Pavel's dad had told him the grinders were criminals, subhuman. "Your dad was wrong. You've lived with them for months now. They're the same as us."

He snorted. "You think whatever you want. All I know is that once we get to Earth, a sure way to get us all killed is to get caught with grinder tattoos."

"Fine," I said, gritting my teeth. "Don't get one. But we are going to be cooped up together for weeks in that transport. Grow. Up."

I stormed back inside, where Darcy was getting her tiny *M* tattoo. Therese was hugging her, and Elena held her hand tenderly. But I could tell that there was no need. Darcy was staring straight ahead, immobile, her lips pursed. There was no trace left of the scared little girl I'd saved from our burning core-scraper.

Chapter Four
Escape

The force of liftoff makes your stomach feel like it's trying to fight its way up your throat. It's both exhilarating and scary. Those emotions joined the profound sadness I felt.

I'd stuck the picture Darcy had drawn for her sixth birthday onto the dashboard. I stared at it now. It was one of the few things I was keeping from Perses. And it was much more than an image of a cake and candles.

In some ways it was all I was going to have left of Perses. A memento of one brief moment when Darcy had still believed in me, talked to me. It was drawn on a piece of paper our parents had brought to Perses when they'd believed in the Great Mission. When I'd believed in the Great Mission.

Darcy had used one of my pens to try to make the darkness of living underground a little brighter.

And, like us, this improbable, fragile piece of paper had survived bombings, fires, Thatcher. I reached out to touch it, but the force of liftoff kept my hands pinned to my chair.

Somewhere below, as the thrusters carried us past the veil of Perses' atmosphere, Therese and Darcy were watching the trail burning against the night sky. Once we were gone they would head south, to what was left of the farming zone. To wait.

As we'd boarded the transport, Darcy had hugged everyone but me, then taken Therese's hand and turned away.

That hurt more than any tattoo.

Unconsciously, I rubbed my arm, still tender, and stared at the picture.

There were now only five of us left. Elena, Fatima, Pavel, Mandeep, and me. There was enough food, water, and supplies to last us through a one-way trip to Earth. At least I hoped so.

The transport broke through the atmosphere. The stars were crisp and clear. They seemed so bright they could burn a hole through the windows.

Elena, sitting next to me, gave a loud whoop. She'd been practicing firing all the rockets for days, making sure the sequence was right but never igniting the precious fuel. Now all that practice had paid off and we were streaking toward space. I felt the undeniable thrill of being on a ship again.

"Told you it was like riding a bicycle," Elena said, straining to turn her head toward me, a huge grin on her face.

I gave her a thumbs-up.

"Trajectory looks good too," Elena said. "We'll be at your apex point in just a few minutes. And the fuel levels are perfect. Nice work, math geek!"

I smiled, only for a second. We were still fighting gravity, with more weight than I'd wanted on board.

The extra weight was my digger.

Pavel had transferred the video of Thatcher's execution of Nazeem onto the ship's computers. But at the last minute, just to be safe, we'd decided to drive the digger, with the original file, into the cargo hold.

Even a slight miscalculation in weight would cost us some fuel now. Once we were in the vacuum of space, ion thrusters would take over, pushing us toward Earth. But it was good old-fashioned rocket fuel that would make this part of the journey work, or fail spectacularly. We'd left a bunch of empty crates and boxes on Perses, but I was only guessing about the trade-off.

I tried not to think about it. I failed.

"Everything's good so far," Elena said, closely monitoring the instrument panel on the ship's dashboard.

I looked out the window. The stars were growing more numerous and incredible every second. It was a tapestry of light. My spirits lifted, ever so slightly, as I caught sight of Earth, a small blue dot far to our right.

"Approaching apex, Fearless Leader. I hope you're right about this next bit."

Elena flipped a switch on the console and the thrusters turned off. Our speed gradually reduced until we came to an almost full stop. Suddenly weightless, our feet and hands began to float. Pavel chuckled from his seat behind us. "This feels so weird," he said.

Within moments, the faintest gravitational pull began to take hold, luring the ship back toward the planet's surface like a tug on a kite string.

"Hit the starboard thrusters," I said.

Elena was already pressing the button.

Small bursts of gas escaped the hull to our left, the force pushing us. We began to turn back toward Perses.

I stared intently at one gauge on the console as its

blue numbers began to rise. 15, 20, 35. Our angle of re-entry.

Perses came into view. I hadn't seen it from this distance since the day we'd arrived.

The planet shimmered—a mix of red, blue, and green. From this height we could see that more and more of the surface was beginning to respond to the terra-forming. Lakes were appearing where there had only been craters. The farming zone, visible as a narrow strip across the equator, was growing wider.

The scars from the attacks, bombings, battles . . . they all seemed to disappear from this distance. It seemed so peaceful. So beautiful. My lips trembled.

"We'll be back," I said, though I didn't know why.

"Let's hope that doesn't happen in the next five minutes," Fatima yelled.

The numbers began to scroll closer and closer to 95 degrees. I closed my eyes and gave a silent wish that all those sleepless nights and never-ending calculations would pay off.

"95," Elena called.

"Opposing thrusters," I said. Elena fired them and we straightened out. The console display stopped at 95 degrees, and it stayed.

"Rear thrusters," I said. There was no need to actually

give instructions—we'd gone over the sequence dozens of times—but it helped me feel useful.

"Aye aye, captain," Elena said.

She fired them and Perses began to grow larger and larger as we sped downward. It looked like we were heading straight for it. The indicator stayed locked on 95 degrees from the angle of our original ascent.

Flashes of light streaked off the hull as we skimmed along the outer surface of the atmosphere. Our velocity climbed as we fell faster and faster.

The ship began to shake as the force of Perses' gravity threatened to tear us apart.

"We're going to crash!" Mandeep yelled.

Pavel screamed so loud my ears almost burst. "You idiot! I knew it! We're going to die in this stupid thing!"

"No. We're not!" I called back. "Just hold on tight. Just a few more minutes." I hoped I sounded more confident than I felt.

Those minutes seemed like hours.

We shook and shook. The temperature of the ship's exterior continued to rise. More flashes of light streaked across the hull.

I tried to focus my shaking eyes on the console but the numbers danced so much I felt ill. I looked left, a last look at Perses out the bridge window. I wished

I hadn't. Clouds swirled on the far side of the planet, illuminated by flashes of lightning. It was an enormous storm.

Perses was still waking up. And we'd just left two of our group down there, alone. Who was in more immediate danger? Therese and Darcy? Or us?

Finally, just as it seemed like the ship was going to break apart, Perses' surface disappeared from view and we shot back out into space, now moving, and spinning, incredibly fast.

It was dizzying to look at the stars.

The indicator was stuck at 96 degrees, exactly the exit angle we'd hoped for. I felt a rush of pride and relief . . . until I remembered the storm.

"On our way!" Elena yelled.

There were loud cheers as we began our journey away from Perses. Even from Pavel, the hypocrite.

I wasn't cheering.

The image of Darcy and Therese caught in some giant storm took hold in my imagination. I had made a vow to never leave anyone behind. I still hadn't reconciled that promise with my decision to do that now.

But as the gravity began to disappear and my body strained to be free of the seat restraints, I knew there was no turning back.

Chapter Five
Tedium

Space is beautiful, haunting, amazing. Space travel, on the other hand, can be incredibly boring. Even for a nerd like me. Now that we were on our way, the days were spent in a mixture of almost unbearable anxiety and exhaustion.

We did our best to cope, but after months of fighting, hiding, and running, all this quiet was creepy.

Mandeep had found a metal backgammon game buried somewhere in a locker—there was a table in the dining room that was magnetic—and she and the others started a backgammon tournament. Once in a while she would end up with a triple-digit lead, and they'd pay her in chocolate or energy bars. Then they'd start all over again.

I spent most of my time watching the rotation of the visible universe, thinking about what was happening to Therese and Darcy back on Perses, and what would happen to us once we landed on Earth.

"Doesn't staring at that make you sick?" Elena's voice surprised me. She was standing beside me, her hand suddenly on my shoulder.

"When did you get here?"

"I've been watching you for about ten minutes. You are totally zoned out."

"Just thinking," I said. "Spinning stars seem to help."

"Mesmerizing."

"Hmm," I said.

We stared out the window in silence for a few minutes.

"You're done with backgammon?" I asked.

"Done with losing at backgammon. I thought I'd see if you wanted to take my spot at the table."

"No. Thanks."

She took her seat and pushed a button. A screen lowered, covering her half of the window. "I know the rotation gives us some semblance of gravity here inside the ship, but it makes me woozy."

I shrugged. "You get used to it." The blue dot—the Earth—was now smack-dab in the center of our path. Was it getting bigger? Barely. "And it's kind of peaceful."

I looked over at Elena, who was staring at me, clearly concerned, her eyebrows furrowed.

"You know, Chris, we're basically on autopilot for, like, a month. If you don't want to play games, you should get some sleep. Or go read a book. There's a great digital library here on board."

I grunted noncommittally and turned back to the stars.

Elena seemed determined to keep my mind occupied. "I read a book on sleeping patterns in extreme conditions."

"Fascinating," I mumbled, un-fascinated.

"It was! There's some seriously weird stuff in there, like how to adapt to mountaintop camps, blizzards, being in submarines, heat waves . . . I guess it does makes sense to have it on board, for reference."

"I guess," I said, still watching the stars spinning.

"Apparently there were these shepherds that would hibernate during winters."

"German shepherds?"

"No. Humans. Real shepherds, with sheep and stuff."

"Okay," I said, not sure why she was telling me this.

"And these guys were French, not German. Somehow they changed their internal rhythms to mimic their animals'. The sheep would hunker down and sleep whole days in a row in winter, so the shepherds would too."

I shrugged again, only partially paying attention.

"Then there are these sleep chambers they used for deep space travel."

"I know about those. From before modern ships got high-speed ion thrusters."

"Much faster."

"There was that ship my mom used to talk about. The *Endeavor*. It went out on some decade-long journey to Pluto. It was a one-way trip, so the scientists slept for years after they'd left Earth."

"But when they woke up, they were still young enough to run the experiments. That's in the book too."

"They sent back incredible data for years. Then they returned to the chambers . . . and died, buried forever in space."

"Maybe a chamber like that would work for you."

"Nice," I said, frowning.

"I meant for sleeping." She laughed.

"Look. It's not that I want to stay awake. I just can't stop my mind from spinning around."

"Like the stars."

There was a cheer from back in the mess hall. "Sounds like Pavel has miraculously beaten Mandeep at backgammon," Elena said. "Or she let him."

"How many games have they played?"

"We stopped keeping track at around three thousand."

I stared back out the window. Earth still hadn't grown perceptibly bigger.

"You know what they say about a watched pot?" Elena said.

"We're getting closer. I just wish it looked like it."

Elena got out of her seat. "You know there's nothing we can do right now, right, Chris? Worrying about Darcy isn't going to help her. Therese is a pro. They'll be fine. Worrying about what happens in a month when we get to Earth isn't going to help either."

I grunted.

She gave my arm a squeeze. "Okay. Well, I'm off to the cargo hold. I found these big metal shipping containers with handles. They make great free weights. Going to do some workouts." She flexed her biceps and kissed each.

"You are one of a kind," I said.

"Don't you ever forget it, Fearless Leader." She winked at me and then walked away. I turned and watched her go. Elena was partially right. There was nothing I could do right now.

But there was a lot I could *plan* to do. And I needed to be ready for whatever happened on Earth. Elena walked out the door and I slumped forward, my head in my hands.

Was I doing the right thing? I was haunted by moments of incredible doubt. I had slipped up with Thatcher, been fooled into a trap that left Julio dead and me a prisoner. Darcy didn't even trust me enough to say goodbye. What kind of a leader was I?

In my darkest thoughts, my latest plan seemed absolutely stupid. Yes, we were on our way to Earth. What exactly were we supposed to do? The Oracle—our only friend back on Earth—was gone, probably dead. She'd sent one last message, not even coded, telling us our receiving beacon was a bomb, and then disappeared. I felt in my gut she'd risked telling us that because she was about to be killed by Thatcher's goons.

Those same goons were still in charge of the defensive perimeter around Earth. They might attack and blow us up as soon as we appeared. Or we might slip through, thanks to the element of surprise. No one knew we were coming, as far as I knew, and we were on a small ship.

But if we did slip past them, then what? Elena had proven she could blast off in the transport and I was convinced she could land it. But where? We needed somewhere people weren't going to be ready to kill us.

How many people supported Thatcher back on Earth? Was there a safe place to land?

My doubts fought a constant battle with my plans and hopes.

Worse, the doubts in my head were always in Thatcher's voice. The voice he'd used when he was torturing me, telling me I'd been a horrible leader. That my actions had led to everyone's deaths. That I was putting my friends, and the Earth, in grave danger. I knew it was all lies. But they were lies that, despite myself, I had let take hold.

Pavel yelled again and began taunting Mandeep and Fatima with some obnoxious cheer.

I leaned back in my chair. The Earth was getting bigger. I was sure of it. I stared at it. My lids got heavier. The heavens spun. Sleep finally took me, and I spent a restless few hours tossing and turning, beset by nightmarish images of Darcy and Therese trapped in a hurricane.

Chapter Six
Inhale

Tap. Tap. Tap. All our old divisions widened under the stress and boredom. Pavel seemed to grow angrier the closer we got to Earth.

Tap. Tap. Tap.

We were sitting on the bridge and trying to have a meeting, the Earth now a larger dot on the horizon, slightly bigger and brighter than a star.

Tap. Tap. Tap. Pavel tapped his fingers steadily on the top of his chair. After every sixty, he called out, "One minute closer to Earth." He seemed to delight in annoying people, especially me.

Tap. Tap. Tap.

"One minute closer to Earth!" he yelled.

I did my best to ignore him, again. Instead, I looked at the others.

"We need to be more careful with the supplies."

"I thought we were sticking to the schedule," Mandeep said.

"We have been, roughly. But maybe I made some mistake in the inventory. The bottom line is that we need to cut back. Landing on Earth weak and famished is not a good idea."

Tap. Tap. Tap.

"Maybe if we get rid of one mouth to feed . . ." Fatima suggested under her breath, quickly glancing at Pavel.

"Not funny," I said. It was actually pretty funny, but I didn't think encouraging Fatima was going to help her get along with Pavel, or vice versa.

Tap. Tap. Tap.

The passion for backgammon had faded. The library had been pretty much exhausted.

Tap. Tap. "One more stupid minute . . ."

"We get it," Fatima said. "Now knock it off."

Pavel ignored her. " . . . Closer to Earth." *Tap. Tap. Tap.*

Fatima clenched her fists and closed her eyes. Her lips moved as she quietly counted to ten.

"See, you're keeping track too," Pavel said, smirking.

"I didn't know you grinders could count that high."

She was up like a shot, but so was I, jumping between them.

"I'm sick of you using *grinder* like it's a curse word."

"Isn't it?" Pavel said. They tried to get at each other through me.

"That's enough," I said.

Suddenly the whole scene began to swim. Little streaks of light passed in front of my eyes, white, then red. I heard someone gasp, then . . . nothing.

I woke up on the floor. Elena was slapping my face. "Chris! Wake up!"

My eyes opened. Elena smiled, relief in her eyes. Fatima came up beside her.

"That was scary," she said. "You okay?"

"I think so," I said, getting up on my elbows. "What happened? Did I get punched?"

"You blacked out," Mandeep said.

Pavel seemed less concerned. He stood with his back to the wall, now counting the passing seconds out loud. "Tick. Tick. Tick."

"Blacked out?"

Mandeep nodded.

"How? I got sleep last night. Well, some. I ate. I had some water . . ." I hadn't even been feeling sick. Maybe a little light-headed, but it was hard not to be in space.

"That's not the only way to black out," Elena said, standing up.

Almost on cue, her head began to loll to the side. Mandeep caught her.

"Head rush," Elena said. "Stood up too fast."

"No. It think it's caused by low oxygen," Mandeep said. "Remember those briefings they gave us on the flight to Perses?"

Every stage of our space flight to Perses—passing the moon, heading to interplanetary space, approaching Perses—had come with a safety demonstration: a video showing the signs of oxygen deprivation. Weakness. Dizziness. Blacking out. We were supposed to limit our activity during high-demand parts of the day to make sure the oxygen supply didn't get overtaxed.

If you felt dizzy or blacked out, it could mean that there was a leak or a malfunction in the oxygen generation unit. No spaceship carries enough oxygen to last even a few hours in space. Instead, it is equipped with systems that take all the available water, including everything from passengers' sweat to their bathroom waste, and extract its oxygen to pump it back into the ship.

"Low oxygen?" I was perplexed. I hadn't forgotten

about the video. It just hadn't clicked in because I'd been checking the levels the entire trip. The supply in the tanks hadn't wavered.

I sat down in my chair and called up the diagnostics screen on the console.

Sure enough, the actual levels of CO_2 in the air were spiking too high, and the oxygen levels were too low. Maybe it was all the vigorous card playing, plus Elena's workouts?

Or maybe it was the fact I was making all of this up as I went along, and really I had no idea how to set oxygen levels on a spaceship. I hung my head. Another mistake that was my fault.

Pavel agreed.

"You screw up the math on the food AND the breathing stuff, Nichols? Makes me feel confident about the rest of your plan. Is there an escape pod? Oh wait, this IS the escape pod."

I gritted my teeth. Why didn't HE black out? Why did he even come on this trip?

As if reading my mind, Fatima said, "You can still leave, Pavel. The airlock door is just outside the bridge."

An image of Pavel flying through space danced across my eyes and I smiled. Then I shook my head. This was not a good thought to entertain.

Cabin fever. It could make you imagine things. *Concentrate,* I told myself.

"Okay. We're somehow using up too much of the oxygen. New plan. I can direct the oxygen to specific parts of the ship. So . . . from now on we stay in one room at a time. Together."

Mandeep groaned.

Fatima glared at Pavel. Pavel glared at Fatima. *This could be more dangerous than oxygen deprivation,* I thought.

Elena looked at me like I was crazy.

I pushed another button and the bridge door closed.

There was an audible hiss as a rush of oxygen came in through the vent. My mood, my energy level, instantly lifted.

It was like magic.

Even the others seemed to relax their shoulders. "Where did you take the oxygen from?" Elena asked. I knew what she was asking.

"Sorry. No workouts for a while. The cargo hold is just too big a space to waste this on."

Elena sat grumpily in her chair.

"I feel like a prisoner," she said.

I couldn't disagree.

Tap. Tap. Tap.

"Pavel, can you please stop that stupid tapping?" I said.

"It's not me, jerk," Pavel said.

I looked over my shoulder. Pavel was standing still. His hands at his sides. No one else was moving either.

The tapping started up again.

We looked up at the ceiling.

The sound was coming from the ventilation duct.

And it was getting louder.

Chapter Seven
Exhale

Tap. Tap. Tap. It grew louder by the second, echoing, growing closer. *Tap. Tap. Tap.*

"Maybe it's the air ducts cooling," Pavel said. "That used to happen sometimes on Perses when the AC turned off at night."

"Maybe," I said. "But it never sounded like it was moving."

"And that was more of a clicking noise," Elena said.

Pavel shrugged, either in agreement or indifference. "That's what I think it is." But he continued to stare at the vent.

The sound grew louder. As it did, it sounded heavier and was joined by a scraping sound, like something being dragged across metal. *Bump. Scritch. Bump.*

"Something might be caught in there, like a loose piece of the vent or something," Fatima said. "Maybe it's getting moved around by the different air flow?"

"But why is the sound so regular?" Mandeep asked. She took a step backward.

Elena narrowed her eyes and stepped forward, her hands balled into fists.

"Could be some rat that stayed on board," Pavel said, apparently now changing his mind. "It's scurrying or something?"

"Not sure that's possible," I said. "There were definitely no rats on Perses."

Bump. Scritch. Bump.

"This is big," Mandeep said. "Sounds more like a bear."

A horrible thought occurred to me. Maybe the Landers had robots, or even mobile bombs, on board, just in case someone tried to hijack the transport ship.

We were still days away from even trying to contact Earth via our short-range communications, but maybe this was something that could be activated remotely, long-distance, like the beacon our parents had hidden on Perses?

Or maybe this was just more fantasy conjured up by the thin air?

There was a final, louder, thump, a crash of metal from the bedroom outside the bridge door, a loud bump, and then . . . silence.

"That was close," Fatima said.

I held my hand up to the vent. The air continued to flow, but more weakly. "If something had been caught in the draft, it might have hit a weak joint in the ductwork and broken through."

"Maybe," Elena said. "But whatever it is, it's somewhere out there." She pointed at the door.

"We need to take a look," Fatima said, not moving.

We all stared at the door, rooted to the spot, almost as if we expected it to open and dreaded that it might.

"What about it, Fearless?" Pavel sneered.

I took a deep breath and made my way to the door. I pressed my ear against it. All I could make out was the sound of my own heart, beating fast and loud. I'm not sure what else I was expecting to hear, but either the cabin door was too thick for sound to come through, or everything on the other side was still.

I stood up straight, reached for the panel to the right of the door, and pressed the button.

I held my breath as the door slid open with a tiny *whoosh.*

Red beacon lights flashed on and off. The glow gave

the scene an eerie feel, like that first night in the mining tunnels on Perses. The sleeping quarters appeared empty.

I stepped into the gloom.

To my left, the exposed pipes and lockers of the sleeping quarters were barely visible in the shadows. To my right, the door to the outside airlock glowed in the red light. Just beyond that was the unforgiving vacuum of space. If that door opened, we'd be sucked out in a millisecond. The image of Pavel floating in space, lifeless, motionless, *quiet*, swam in front of my eyes again. Not good thoughts, but I just couldn't seem to shake them. The oxygen levels in this room must not have caught up to the bridge yet. At least that's what I told myself.

I stepped farther out, grabbed a helmet, and turned on the light. I scanned the room, walking cautiously. I could hear footsteps behind me as the others followed slowly. I wanted to look confident but I was shaking.

I swept my head from side to side but saw nothing out of the ordinary. That didn't stop the chill that ran up my spine.

Suddenly, something brushed my arm.

"AHHH!" I yelled and jumped back about ten feet, slipping and landing on my butt.

I scrambled to stand up, but Pavel was already shining his light on the culprit. It was just one of our overalls, hanging by a hook and swaying in the low gravity. I'd walked right into it.

"You sounded just like a chicken," he said, laughing.

"Ha ha," I said. I walked over to the overalls. They didn't look so scary now. I grabbed the arm and shook it. "You'd have been scared too," I said, grumping a little.

"You did sound a little like a chicken," Elena said, chuckling. Fatima and Mandeep smiled, their faces glowing in the low light.

"We still don't know what the sound was," I pointed out. They stopped laughing. I let go of the arm. It fell back against the metal locker, the zipper tapping the door.

At that moment the lights came back up, temporarily blinding us.

"The oxygen levels must be back to normal in here," Fatima said.

I flicked off my headlamp and blinked until my eyes adjusted.

The beds were untouched and (except for Pavel's) tidy.

"See, everything is hunky-dory," Pavel said. His stomach gave an audible growl. "Dinnertime," he said.

He strutted past me to the dining hall. He pressed a button and the door slid aside.

The dining room was still dark, still cut off from the oxygen supply. The red safety lights reflected off the metal tabletops, looking like pools of blood. Pavel stopped in the doorway.

"Pavel, wait until the lights turn on," I said.

"What's the matter?" he said. "Still chicken?"

"Just for once, listen to me."

He turned and glared.

"Go to hell, Nichols," he said. He stepped inside backward, waving.

The door began to slide shut just as I saw the missing air vent in the ductwork above the door and the fresh drops of blood on the floor below it.

Pavel screamed, the sound instantly cut off by the closing door.

"What the . . . ?" Elena said.

"Pavel?" I called.

No response.

I pounded on the metal door. It wouldn't budge.

"Pavel!" I yelled. "This isn't funny!"

The door slid open just a crack.

A voice spoke from the other side.

His voice.

Gravelly, hoarse, evil.

"If you ever want to see your friend alive, Nichols, you'll step aside and let me onto the bridge."

Thatcher.

I was too shocked to speak. My knees buckled. How was he even alive? How had he made it onto the ship?

"You will go back and turn the oxygen back on in this entire ship, including this room. Then I'll give you ten minutes to clear out and leave the bridge door open. If you refuse, he dies."

The door slid shut.

I pounded again and again, but it would not open.

Chapter Eight
Vacuum

"He's bluffing," Elena said. We were all back on the bridge, door closed, debating what to do next. I didn't need Pavel's ticking and tapping to know that time was passing way too fast.

"How can he be bluffing?" Fatima asked.

"He can't kill Pavel. That's his only bargaining chip. He needs a hostage."

"He's also holed up in the only place where we have food," Mandeep said. "He could stay locked in there and we'll starve out here. So the food works just as well as a hostage."

There were so many questions going through my head. "Why didn't he just come out with Pavel right away?"

Elena peered at the door like she was trying to see through it. "He's probably tying him up. Knocked him out and needs some time to get him ready so that he can't wiggle free or fight back."

"How is Thatcher even alive?" I said, shaking my head in disbelief.

"We'll ask him, before we send him floating out into space," Fatima said.

"And how did he get inside?"

Elena pointed to the vent. "Doesn't matter. He got in here at some point and was holed up in the ducts like a rat in a nest. When we turned off the oxygen to the rest of the ship, he could tell."

"The emergency lights," I said. They had come on in the places where we'd cut the air supply. That was how Thatcher had known he was about to lose his breathable air.

"Wait. Why don't we just turn off the oxygen supply to the dining room again?"

"No," I said. "If he sees the emergency lights go on, he'll just kill Pavel on the spot." I moaned and ran my hands through my hair. This couldn't be happening.

"How do we know Pavel is even still alive?" Fatima asked.

"Yeah," Mandeep said. "Did you see him or hear him?"

I shook my head. "All I heard was Thatcher. The room was dark, just that blinking red light."

I thought of all the fantasies I'd had of shoving Pavel out into space. The guilt bore into me. "We have to assume he's alive."

Elena took a deep breath. "Okay, then next question. Why does Thatcher want to be on the bridge? Answer: He wants to decide how we get to Earth, and who we meet when we get there. He wants to save his own skin and make sure that we aren't able to damage his reputation."

"Why didn't he kill us all already?" Mandeep asked. "He could have taken over the ship and dumped us in space, and no one would ever know what really happened."

"Good points," Elena said. She chewed on her lip for a moment before answering. "He's still injured. I remember thinking that there was a lot of blood after that fight between you and Pavel."

"You mean he snuck on when we were fighting?"

Elena gave a small nod. "But he was incredibly weak. Too weak to risk a fight. Mandeep, remember you complained that they'd used way too much of the supplies?"

"We're almost out of surgical tape and gauze."

I hadn't thought much about that at the time. I'd been

too preoccupied with Darcy. But there was no way we'd gone through all those medical supplies in the few days we'd been on the ship.

I punched my injured hand against my other palm. I'd done it again, let down my guard at exactly the wrong time. "Thatcher stole them and then hid in the ship, waiting and recovering."

"He did plan to kill us," Fatima said. "Eventually."

I stared at the vent. "And then we turned off the oxygen before he was ready. It was a stroke of luck that forced him out."

Fatima looked disgusted. "So he was waiting to recover. Then he was going to steal some knives or something else before coming after us."

"Knives for sure." Elena nodded. "He couldn't risk firing a blaster inside a spaceship or we'd all get sucked out a hole. Him included."

"And the mess hall and kitchen have plenty of knives," Mandeep said.

I stared at the vent. "But there's one thing we have that Thatcher doesn't," I said. "Blankets."

Chapter Nine

Twisted

I knocked on the door to the dining room.

"Thatcher. We're here. The bridge is open and clear. Now come out. We won't stand in your way."

I stepped back and waited. The others were lined up behind me, hugging the wall of the bedroom, clearly visible from the doorway.

There was no movement. "No tricks," I shouted.

The door opened a crack.

Pavel stepped through, if you could call his shuffling movement a step. His hands were bound behind his back with torn strips of his own shirt, the laces of his boots tied together. His face was swollen and bruised. Elena had been right. Thatcher needed him as a hostage.

Pavel stared at the ground, a low moan the only sound from his swollen lips.

"Oh, Pavel," Mandeep said, and she took a step toward him.

"Stop!" Thatcher yelled from the darkness. He held a long knife into the light, then pulled it back. Pavel gave a yelp and lurched forward. "Any more sudden moves and the knife that's against his back will go all the way through it. Then I'll come for everyone else. I might die, but so will all of you."

Mandeep walked back to the wall. Pavel gave her a wary glance, then grimaced in pain as he took another tentative step away from the door.

Thatcher emerged from the darkness. I cringed. He was stooped over, clearly in pain from broken bones or worse. His back was bent awkwardly, as if his spine had been twisted the wrong way and then jammed back together again. His face was a mass of cuts and bruises. His right eye was swollen so much it was hard to believe he could see out of it. Pavel looked healthy by comparison.

Thatcher took a step forward, his gnarled left hand now resting on Pavel's left shoulder. His right hand and knife remained hidden behind Pavel's back.

One leg moved at an odd angle, seemingly

independent from the rest of his body. His left forearm was wrapped over and over in Mandeep's precious medical tape and gauze.

He gave a hollow laugh. "Yes, take a good, long look, you little piece of excrement," he said, staring straight at me. "This is what you've done to me. That little bomb you threw down the hole almost finished me off."

"That was me, Thatcher," Elena said.

Thatcher kept his eyes locked on mine. "But there were lots of little side tunnels down there. I was burned, cracked, but I survived. And I watched. And I waited. And then you looked away. I knew you would. That little brat ran, and you couldn't help but follow. Sent everyone else off too. For what? A useless girl." He spat on the floor. "Weakness, Nichols. That's always your downfall."

I'd been subjected to this before—Thatcher twisting the truth, trying to make everything seem like my fault, a result of my failings.

"That's not true," I said. But the doubts began to creep in. My head began to fill with images of dead friends. *My fault,* I thought.

"Chris, ignore him," Fatima said.

Thatcher made a show of sniffing the air. "Ah, a grinder. I thought I smelled one on the ship."

Fatima flinched, her eyes narrowing. Thatcher smirked.

"I notice your grinder friend stayed behind and left you to die here in space. No one ever said grinders aren't shrewd. She'll have that brat working as her slave, or out of the way, in no time. She's probably killed her already."

"You just keep spinning those lies," Fatima said. She took a step forward, fists at her side.

Thatcher chuckled. "Maybe you *want* me to kill this one?" Pavel yelped again as Thatcher jabbed at his back. "He's certainly no lover of grinders."

Fatima stopped.

"He's told me all about how you've tried to shove Nichols aside, take over."

"You're crazy," I said.

Did Thatcher believe that? Did Pavel? I did not.

Thatcher continued to push Pavel ahead of him, shuffling across the floor so they were both facing us. They passed me and I realized with horror that most of his right foot had been blown off. What was left covered in rags.

"Not a pretty sight, I know," Thatcher said, following my gaze. He stopped and scowled.

This wasn't good. I needed him to move more

quickly. I could already feel my head beginning to swim. Mandeep, to my right, began to slip. Her knees buckled and she leaned back against the wall to steady herself.

"You don't need Pavel anymore," I said. "The bridge door is open. Just leave him here so we can take care of him."

"I'm crippled, not stupid," Thatcher hissed. "He comes with me all the way to the door."

Pavel caught my eye. I wanted to give him a look of reassurance, that this would all work out fine, but his eyes were like glass. His body began to sway. *Oh no,* I thought.

"Thatcher, he's lost too much blood. Take me instead." I stepped forward. Pavel, almost on cue, sagged in Thatcher's grip, his knees banging down onto the floor.

Thatcher kicked him aside, then held the knife out in front of him. A patch of red was forming on the back of Pavel's shirt.

"Don't anyone else move," Thatcher said. He motioned for me to come closer, then reached out and grabbed my arm. Despite his injuries, he was incredibly strong, and he swung me around, pressing the knife against my neck. The blade bit my skin.

"How does that feel, Nichols?" he said, pressing the knife again, cutting me.

"If you kill me, they'll kill you," I said.

"I know. But I don't plan to kill you . . . yet," Thatcher said.

"Then let them help Pavel."

"Nobody moves. Not until I'm safely on the bridge."

He'd finally given me the excuse I needed. "Then move," I said, pushing with my legs to make us both go faster.

The others stayed motionless, but I could see each of them beginning to wobble. How was Thatcher able to stay upright?

Finally, he reached the door. He took the knife from my neck and let me go. I stood up straight and turned to look at him.

Thatcher's face twisted into an evil grin. "Join your friends," he said. "You can all die together."

Then, before I could move, he leaned forward and sliced at my chest. I stumbled back, my hands now red with blood.

Chapter Ten
Gasp

Thatcher lifted his head and laughed. Then he pushed the button and the door closed.

I spun around, the world swimming, turning blurry.

Mandeep looked at my hands and screamed.

At least I think she screamed. It was hard to tell through the mask she had just put on. I fell to the ground. Elena and Fatima rushed toward me. Everything began to spin.

The next thing I remembered was Mandeep hovering over me in a fog. No, not fog . . . the mist of my own breath on the inside of my mask. She was saying something. I couldn't hear her voice, but I could see her lips forming my name.

"Chris. Chris." She wasn't wearing a mask anymore. That meant things were either going well or horribly wrong.

"Is he down?" I asked weakly.

She cocked her head and leaned her ear closer.

I repeated my question, as loudly as I could.

Mandeep took a second to register what I'd said, then she straightened up and nodded.

I tried to sit up, but the effort sent a screaming pain through my body.

Mandeep rested her hands on my shoulders and settled me down. I could tell I was on the floor near the dining room.

She gingerly took off the mask. "I think your lungs have recovered enough," she said.

I took a deep breath of the air in the cabin. I was lying on my own bed, my back propped up by some pillows.

"Better?" she asked.

I nodded. "What happened?"

"You lost some blood. Luckily Thatcher didn't hit any vital organs, as far as I can tell."

"That's reassuring." I grimaced.

"But you've got some nasty stitches and some sore muscles. So stay put for a second." Mandeep walked away.

"But what happened?"

Elena's head popped into view. "We found him passed out in a heap, as you'd predicted." She jerked her head to the right.

With the mask off, I could move my head just enough to see Thatcher in the dining room, tied and taped to a chair. His hands were behind his back, and a piece of tape covered his mouth. His head hung low, not moving. He wasn't wearing a mask.

"Is he dead?"

Elena frowned. "Sadly, no. We put an oxygen mask on him after we tied him up. He seems fine breathing on his own now so we took it off. The guy is built like an ox. Mandeep is keeping an eye on him."

"Pavel okay?" I asked.

Elena nodded. "He's sleeping right now. Not talking much when he's awake. He might be concussed, or he might just be miserable. Thatcher clubbed him pretty hard." She leaned in closer and put her hand on my arm. "Thatcher was beating information out of him." She turned and glared at Thatcher, her eyes blazing. Her fingers suddenly gripped my arm so tightly I winced. "He's a monster."

"We can't kill him, Elena," I said.

She didn't flinch. I knew I'd guessed her thoughts.

"We're going to take him back to Earth. He's going to stand trial."

"Trial," Elena said with a snort. "He should be dead already."

"Agreed," I said. "But he's not. And he's here." I took a few seconds to frame my thoughts. "You know, this is great news. We have him under our control."

"There's no controlling him. He's like a ticking time bomb."

"He's ours. It could even help us when we get back to Earth."

Elena turned and looked at the gash in my uniform. "Yeah. It's going great so far. Would you also like to ask Pavel his opinion?"

"What I mean is that he's a bargaining chip."

"Bargaining chip? Him?" She looked back at Thatcher. She bit her lip for a few moments, then spoke more slowly, thinking out loud. "You mean in case we get caught and have to make a deal?"

"Bargaining chip, hostage, whatever you want to call it. Yes. And even if it doesn't come to that, Thatcher—alive— might help our credibility when we get back to Earth."

"How?"

"A trial allows us to get everything out in the open, expose him and what he did."

"We don't need him alive to expose what he did."

"No, but with him alive, no one can accuse us of being murderers, or rebels, or of lying or making it all up."

She raised an eyebrow.

I sighed. "Fine, of course they can, and probably will, but having Thatcher there makes it easier to convince people that we are not lying. And that we don't kill our prisoners. We are better than them."

"Horrible points taken." Her eyes met mine. "But you agree that we might reach a point where he becomes more dangerous to us alive."

I paused, then nodded. A number of unspoken possibilities passed between us. I had no doubt of what Elena was capable of. And she was just as aware of my thoughts.

"You're going to talk to him, aren't you?" Elena said, shaking her head.

"He could help us."

She snorted. "Your way, again." She turned to go. "Chris, he can't be trusted. Everything he says is a lie. The only reason I didn't hurl him out of the hatch when you were knocked out is that I knew you'd think it was wrong."

"And do you think I'm wrong?"

Elena stared at Thatcher but didn't answer. "I need to

go help Fatima get the rest of the blankets we jammed into the vents." Then she walked away.

I laid my head back against the pillows and stared straight up. Blocking the CO_2 vents had been yet another all-or-nothing risk. If Thatcher had realized what we'd done—stuffing blankets into the exhaust vents, kicking dangerous CO_2 back into the air supply—he might have attacked us.

Thatcher had the only knife. The rest were in the kitchen. Elena had a blaster hidden in her locker, but Thatcher never gave us a clear shot. And missing would have put a hole in the hull, and gotten us all killed.

Though we might still have risked that, I realized.

There had also been the chance that Thatcher wouldn't succumb to the weak air, and he'd easily be able to take care of a bunch of passed-out kids. I was pretty sure that was his long-term plan. Get to the bridge, seal it off until we suffocated. Then dump us in space and return home, with whatever lie he wanted to tell.

I had a sudden, horrible thought. Elena said Thatcher had used his ten minutes alone with Pavel to get information. Had Pavel told him about the video of Nazeem?

I knew Pavel must be recuperating nearby, but the pain of turning my body to look forced me to stop.

To cheer myself, I imagined the look on Thatcher's face just before he passed out, when he'd realized what we'd done.

He must have searched frantically for an oxygen mask in the bridge. We'd taken them all and hidden them.

Now he was our prisoner.

Still, I needed to convince the others we needed him alive.

Pavel, I was certain, would eventually find his voice and start screaming for revenge.

I got that. I'd seen what Thatcher was capable of. But we were better than Thatcher. Better than his Lander troops. We had to be.

Mandeep came back over and handed me a pill and a cup of water. "I'm rationing the pain killers. You can have this."

I knew what Mandeep meant. She wasn't giving Thatcher any. I swallowed the pill. That little bit of revenge felt pretty damn good.

Chapter Eleven

Cold

After just a day I could stand up reasonably well. My ability to bounce back from injuries was one of the few nice surprises of the past few months. My mother and father would have been shocked. I was more of a book nerd than a jock. Elena used to call me a wimp.

I got up, wincing but mostly okay. Pavel was snoring loudly on the floor nearby.

Everyone else was on the bridge, making sure Thatcher hadn't tampered with anything before he'd passed out. I didn't think he would have—he wanted to make it to Earth as much as we did—but he was also calculating and cruel, so it made sense to be vigilant.

This meant Thatcher and I were as good as alone together. Ironically, the tables had been turned.

I gingerly made my way to the dining room and slid a chair in front of Thatcher, just as he'd slid one in front of me a few weeks before. His eyes rose to meet mine. His lids lowered and even with the tape on his mouth, I could see his jaw tense. He looked like a muzzled pit bull ready to strike.

I leaned across and ripped the tape off his mouth.

"You're all going to die," he snarled.

I made a show of unpeeling a new strip of duct tape off the roll, readying it to put back on his face.

"We need to talk."

"You can't escape your fate. You are going to die." He sounded calm, even though every muscle in his body was twitching with rage, or pain, or both.

I took a deep breath and ripped the tape off the roll.

"If we die, you die."

Thatcher gave a low, hollow laugh, finishing with a hacking cough.

"It's true and you know it," I said.

He relaxed slightly and looked down at his wrapped arms. "I appear to be a captive audience. Enlighten me."

I put down the tape. "Getting this ship home was always a gamble. Our best hope was to slip through the security perimeter unnoticed. Not easy for a transport this size, but not impossible."

"It was impossible. Still is. My people are always watching."

"Too bad. Because unless we can identify ourselves in a way that makes it clear that we're friendly, they'll blow us from the sky. You, tied up on this ship, stubbornly silent, will die the same way we all do. Or am I wrong?"

"That would be the correct protocol for an unidentified ship. For all they know, you're grinders escaped from Perses, planning on crashing the ship into a city somewhere."

"So if we are detected . . ."

"You are doomed."

"Not *you*. *WE*. There's no way for you to get off this ship, the last time I checked, without dying."

"I don't plan on letting that happen." He smirked.

I leaned in close. "You won't be able to stop it from happening. Unless . . ." I paused.

"I give you the security codes you need to get clearance."

"So we need some kind of security codes."

Thatcher narrowed his eyes and glared at me. "Very clever little trick."

"What are they?"

"Are you insane or just naive?" he said. "The second

I hand them over, you and that filthy grinder will chuck me out into space through the airlock."

I shook my head. "I'm weak, remember? There's no way I'd let that happen and you know it. You were pretending to be unconscious, but you were listening when me and El . . . my second-in-command were talking."

"Elena Rosales." He said Elena's name slowly, menacingly, enunciating each syllable. "I know all your names, Christopher Nichols. And what's to stop Elena Rosales and Fatima Carvalho from putting a knife in me when you're not looking?"

I leaned back and folded my arms. "Trust. Friendship. The things that have helped us survive for months now. The things that helped a bunch of grinder and miner kids beat *you*."

Thatcher snorted. "All you've done is prolong your own inevitable death. And by destroying the mission to Perses, you've doomed the Earth to years of privation and destruction. If I'm not there to lead, to keep it all together, it will devolve into utter chaos, and you will be the reason."

Thatcher had said these same words to me when our positions had been reversed: that I'd put the Earth in danger. They still stung. There was some truth in them. Some. That's what makes a lie so powerful, that small grain of truth at the center.

"You started this fight by killing innocent people," I said. "And you are going to pay for it. When we get back to Earth, we'll tell them what you did on Perses."

"And you think they'll believe your word against mine?"

Your *word*. So he didn't know about the video. One more important nugget of information.

"Why wouldn't they believe me? I have the scars to prove we were attacked." I held up my injured hand.

He jerked his head toward my exposed arm, the skin still red from where Mandeep had made the *M* tattoo. "You have the tattoo to prove that you're a grinder. You signed your own death warrant the second you put that on your arm."

"This is a MiNRs tattoo. It's not a brand. It's a bond."

"You think those idiots on Earth will see the difference? Then you're more stupid than you look."

I reached down and grabbed the strip of tape off my pant leg. "They will believe me," I said. "I'll make them." I tried to sound more confident than I felt.

"Then maybe I should die in a battle," Thatcher said, his tone mocking. "It's a more honorable death for a soldier than humiliation and prison."

"Maybe we just tell your troops we've got you on board, a hostage."

"They either won't believe you or they'll wait until

you land, then kill you to save me. They'll find a way. There's no escape, Nichols."

"You could easily die in that kind of attack too."

"I'll take my chances with trained soldiers over a bunch of kids."

This time I smirked. "How did that work out on Perses?"

His smirk turned into a scowl. "You won't get those codes from me."

I stood up. "We'll see what you decide if your troops detect us approaching Earth."

I reached down and placed the new piece of tape across Thatcher's mouth. He glared at me but didn't resist.

I was doing my best to sound and act like I was in control, but I knew I wasn't, not completely.

"Chris?" It was Elena, calling from the doorway to the bridge. Her head popped out. She spied me standing close to Thatcher and cocked an eyebrow.

"All good?" she asked.

"What is it?"

She turned and looked back. I could hear the crackle of static from inside.

"You need to come hear this."

Chapter Twelve
Crackle

The faintest suggestion of a human voice—a woman's?—broke through the static in waves.

"I thought Pavel said we were still too far out to pick anything up."

"He said we could receive but that our transmitter is short-range only, so we can't send anything back. At least not something that would travel much faster than the ship."

I leaned my ear closer to the speaker, as if that would help boost the signal.

"They're probably moving their own transmitter on Earth." It was Pavel's voice. I swung around. He'd woken up and limped his way into the cabin. "It's a shotgun approach. Aim the signal at different places, sweeping the sky. Then stick to the one that works."

"How do they know which one works?"

"When they get an answer back."

The woman's voice came through again, in mid-sentence, slightly more clearly. *"To land in a"*—crackle—*"zone you . . ."* Then it disappeared in static.

"What kind of zone?" Elena asked.

I leaned in close again. "Maybe it's just some standard procedural call for approaching spacecraft?"

Pavel shook his head. "No. They're looking for someone. That's why they're sweeping."

The voice would come back for brief moments, like a fish jumping out of water. We only caught frustrating and increasingly ominous snippets.

"Landing in . . ."

"Must not allow troops . . ."

"Not safe unless . . ."

"Rebels attacking the . . ."

"Look for coordinates matching . . ."

"Armed and willing to . . ."

Then, finally:

"Hello. Do you understand? Hel . . ."

My jaw dropped.

The others' faces told me they felt the same thing: shock and confusion.

I leaped for the radio. "Hello! Hello! Oracle, come in!"

"It won't reach," Pavel said. "We're too far away. But maybe we can figure out where the signal is coming from."

"Okay, do that," I said, getting up from my chair.

Pavel made his way over slowly, wincing. He slid into the chair, his eyes barely open as he fought the pain.

"The signal is strongest from this angle." He pointed to some kind of chart on the view screen. A green triangle throbbed as the signal got clearer.

"Willing to kill on sight . . ."

"So the angle of the signal means it's coming from Earth, instead of the moon or a ship in space." Pavel leaned back. "As we get closer, we should be able to narrow it down more and more."

Then, all of a sudden, the signal stopped.

The low static remained, but the voice didn't return.

"Is she gone?" I asked.

"Possibly. Or they've switched the signal to sweep another part of the sky."

I fell back into one of the other chairs. "The Oracle is alive? Why isn't she using code, or a secret frequency?"

"You blew up the special receiver, remember?" Fatima said. "Not saying that was a bad thing." The beacon receiver had contained the bomb we'd used to blow up Thatcher's ship. Fatima was right, it wasn't a bad thing.

But I'd assumed that we'd never be able to reach the Oracle again without it. In fact, we'd all assumed the Oracle had been killed.

Elena turned down the volume on the speaker. "She's taking a big risk sending non-encrypted messages over the air like that."

"Must be desperate," Fatima said. "Surely someone would recognize her voice."

"She knows we're coming, at least," I said.

"Or hopes we are," Elena said.

Mandeep gazed out the window. "It sounds like she's trying to help us."

I looked at my notes. We still had two weeks before we'd reach Earth. Two weeks of keeping Thatcher a prisoner. Two weeks of trying not to get on each other's nerves.

Maybe if we could connect with the Oracle, we could find out what to do once we got close. Maybe we could get clearance codes. She'd known the codes to get into the transport. She'd know where we should land and who we needed to show the video to. Who would help us destroy the maze of lies that Thatcher had been constructing for years.

"Do we risk answering her once we're in range?" Mandeep asked.

I was confused. "What do you mean?"

"I mean that if we respond to her, she'll know exactly where we are, right?"

"And so will anyone else who's listening," Pavel said.

The hope I'd felt just a second earlier evaporated.

"And I sure as heck didn't like the sound of 'armed and willing to . . .'" Pavel said.

Elena cut him off, more excited than deflated. "What do you think she meant about 'rebels'?"

Fatima answered. "We've been out of contact for weeks. But the news of Thatcher's 'death' on Perses, and the failure of his mission, must have reached his troops, and his enemies."

We all looked at her.

"The grinders would sense there's a weakness, and an opportunity. The grinders must have risen up."

Chapter Thirteen

Mess

The stars spun and the Earth grew ever bigger and brighter. Music blasted out of the console speakers, ringing throughout the ship. Pavel had found a way to hack into the ship's entertainment system. After playing an emergency video about oxygen levels on repeat for three hours, he'd finally found some music files in the database.

As I sat listening, it struck me as absurd. It had taken us months just to get the stereo working. How were we going to land a spaceship? But I parked my concerns in the back of my mind and added "how to land a ship" to the list of questions we'd ask the Oracle. Or that crucial step could be one more thing I'd demand from Thatcher if he wanted to survive.

Some kind of atonal jazz number came over the speakers, starting off with a loud trumpet blast. I jumped in my seat.

"What the heck is that?"

"It's a trumpet, genius," Pavel called back from somewhere near the beds.

I shook my head as the music calmed down and went back to staring at the Earth.

Elena walked up next to me.

"The DJ sure has eclectic taste," she joked.

"At least it's a nice distraction."

"We close enough yet?"

"Not yet. But soon," I said.

Pavel had said we were now in range to answer back.

Elena put her hands on the console and stared at the Earth. "Should we risk answering the Oracle, even to let her know we're here? Alive?"

I didn't answer. We'd been asking the same questions for days.

The Oracle had swept past us again, twice. The voice—the same woman's voice—had grown sharper, and the message had been stripped bare. Instead of warnings about what awaited us on our return, it simply repeated "Hello, hello," over and over again. That had been our key word when we'd talked on Perses. I was more sure than ever. It had to be her.

"She wised up," Elena suggested. "Doesn't want to risk giving away too much information."

"Or perhaps she's being cautious until she hears back," I said. "Sending only short messages, too short to be traced."

"Pavel says the source is still moving around," Elena said. "Slightly different angles each time."

"Maybe she's on the run," I said.

"Which means she's taking a risk to reach us. And maybe that's a reason to risk talking to her."

"Maybe."

Elena stood up. "I'm going to check on our parasite . . . I mean, prisoner," she said. She gave my shoulder a squeeze and left me alone on the bridge.

I'd talked to Thatcher many more times, each time ending in a stalemate. He refused to give us the access codes to pass through the security perimeter safely— willing to die, he said, rather than become a prisoner on Earth. He vowed we'd die with him in space, or the second we landed on Earth.

"And besides, Nichols," he said, "have you even figured out how you're going to get me to this hypothetical trial you keep yammering on about?"

In my mind, we'd land the ship somewhere safe, then

turn Thatcher and the video over to the authorities. But, as Elena and Fatima kept pointing out, the authorities *were* Thatcher and the people at Melming Mining.

This made contacting the Oracle look like our best option. But if she couldn't offer us a safe place to land, what could we do?

Land in some remote area and then force Thatcher to move? Carry him?

Could we tie him up and leave him while *we* escaped?

Could we afford to let him live if we couldn't take him with us?

For now, he was a strain on our resources, and the more he recovered, the more we could feel the physical menace of his presence.

"All he needs to do is figure out some way to cut those bonds, and we're doomed," Fatima said after watching him glare at her for a full hour.

She wasn't wrong. And as the days dragged on, it became harder and harder to be vigilant. Pavel fell asleep on watch once. Luckily, Thatcher had been sleeping too. Another time, I'd looked away out the window and fallen into a daze watching the spinning stars. When I finally looked back, Thatcher was just a foot away from me. He'd inched forward silently, using just his feet. We kept his legs tied together after that.

Except, of course, we couldn't. Not all the time.

Mandeep, for one, felt it was completely inhumane to keep him from moving. So twice a day we would let him take a small walk. Elena kept a blaster aimed at him while he shuffled around. "I'm a very good shot," she'd say menacingly. "I can hit you and not hit the hull."

We also fed him, but only a tiny bit. I wanted him hungry and weak, and we needed the food more than he did. But still, it cut into our supplies.

And he needed to go to the bathroom. We also *needed* him to go to the bathroom, because the waste filtration system was our only source of oxygen and water.

This had almost led to a mutiny when I'd told Pavel we'd need to take turns "helping him" do his business.

"We are not letting him get his hands free," Elena said. "End of story."

I agreed. "We'll take turns."

Pavel leaped to his feet. "Are you insane?"

Luckily, the ship was equipped with a specially made shower. This, by general consensus, became Thatcher's personal bathroom.

The solution wasn't elegant, but it kept Thatcher from either being unguarded or unbound.

It also meant that all the others refused to use the shower for the remainder of the journey, and the bridge was starting to get very stuffy. You can only get so clean with cloths and pre-wetted swabs. I had made some adjustments to the oxygen flow so we could move around the three main rooms more freely, but the cargo hold was still too big and remained off-limits. This area was also where we discovered Thatcher's rabbit hole. He'd hidden in the ductwork until takeoff, then slid his stolen medical supplies and food into an empty storage trunk along the wall.

The thought of him lying in wait while she'd worked out a few feet away all those weeks made Elena hate him even more.

The music continued to blare, now some classical song. I realized with a start that it was "Venus" from Holst's *The Planets*. It was the song Elena and I were dancing to when the first bombs fell.

"Pavel. How do I shut this thing off?" I yelled over the music.

Pavel yelled back. "Sorry, but His Royal Highness wants to visit the loo. I'll switch jobs with you, though."

"No, thanks," I called. "I'll figure it out."

Pavel said something I couldn't quite hear over the music, but I was pretty sure it was a swear word.

I fiddled around with some switches on the console, but the music continued to play. We were reaching the point of the piece that had been playing when Elena had tried to kiss me. For some reason I felt a rising sense of panic, as if we were back on the dance floor and the Blackout was about to begin, and everyone was about to die all over again. A cold sweat began to pour down my face.

The music continued on. In desperation I lunged at a panel on the far right of the console and yanked a thin black cord out of its socket.

It was stupid. Who knew what that cord controlled.

But the music stopped. The stars continued to spin. The Earth continued to grow larger on the horizon. I hadn't wrecked us.

I sat back in my chair and let out a long breath.

My hands were shaking, the cord dancing like a snake in my grip.

"Dinnertime!" Mandeep called enthusiastically.

The announcement was met with groans. The rations were mostly canned vegetables, beans, and what might once have been meat.

"As soon as we get settled on Earth, I'm ordering the biggest steak you can imagine," Pavel said. I looked out the door. He was just untying Thatcher's legs.

"I'm just having giant desserts non-stop," Elena said dreamily. "Nothing but banana splits and churros. Day after day."

"I'd settle for a nice curry and some naan," Fatima said.

"Yeah. With some chickpeas and lentil stew," Mandeep said. "But I'm afraid dinner tonight is beans. And the leftovers are breakfast tomorrow."

That broke the spell.

Pavel had gotten Thatcher to his feet, his mouth still taped, and they marched off to the bathroom. Elena raised her blaster and followed.

"Save me some beans," she joked.

I hadn't moved, or even bothered to daydream about food.

Fatima poked her head into the bridge. "Don't make us eat this feast without you."

"I'll be there in a minute," I said, still trembling. I was gripped by the memory of Elena's hand in mine, her lips close . . . and then the wrenching pain of a bomb exploding at our feet.

"Chris. You need to come eat," Mandeep called.

"Yes, Doctor Mom," I said under my breath.

I let the cord slip from my hands and stood up.

A squawk of static burst through the speaker, followed by the Oracle's voice.

"Hello. This will be my last transmission. It is not safe. Rebels and Melming troops are fighting. You must

not land without notifying me. I can help, but you must contact me. I'll repeat this one final time." There was a long pause, then: *"Hello. This will be . . ."*

I stood frozen to the spot. Should I respond? Was it a trap? The Oracle had been our only ally, but there were still so many unanswered questions about her.

I looked around the bridge. I was alone. "Fatima?" I called. But she and Mandeep were now in the dining room. Pavel and Elena were with Thatcher.

"It is not safe . . ."

Could my call back be traced? Would answering put us in more danger?

"You must not land without . . ."

My hand hovered over the microphone switch. No matter what I decided, there would be no turning back from the consequences.

This was my call and time was running out.

"You must contact me."

I pressed the button.

"We are here!" That was all. I switched off the microphone, then leaned back and stared at the console as if it were suddenly on fire, about to explode. It was done. Had she heard me?

"I cannot repeat . . ." She stopped. The static settled down. I could almost see the Oracle fine-tuning the

transmitter to lock on to our location. I prayed she was the only one.

"Hello. Remember this. 45. 91. 39. 10. 75. 22. I will repeat one more time. Then I must go to the underground."

She repeated the sequence. I hurried to write it down. But I didn't dare respond again.

"Good luck. Look for me in the underground." Then the signal cut out, replaced by louder static.

I looked down at the paper. 45. 91. 39. 10. 75. 22.

It had to be the security code. She'd given us the code that had got us on this transport. She was now going to help us get through the security barrier surrounding Earth!

Fatima came back with a plate of food. "I figured you didn't want to leave the bridge," she said.

She saw something in my face and stopped. "What happened?"

"Something that changes everything . . . I think."

"You think?"

But before I could explain, we were interrupted by a yell and the sound of a firing blaster.

Chapter Fourteen
Safety Valve

Fatima and I rushed to the doorway just in time to see Thatcher fall to the ground. Elena stood over him, the muzzle of her blaster smoking. She swayed and stumbled, turning toward me, revealing a thick gash on her forehead.

"Elena!" I ran and caught her. Her eyes rolled back in her head. I laid her down on the floor and did my best to stop the blood flow with pressure from my hand. "No no no no no."

"I'll get Mandeep," Fatima said.

But Mandeep was already on her way, drawn out of the kitchen by the noise. As soon as she saw Elena, she pushed me aside and began spraying the wound with some kind of foam. "It will stop the bleeding. But give me some room. NOW."

I stood up, my shirt front wet with blood. I turned to where Thatcher lay on the floor. He wasn't dead. He was moaning, writhing in pain. Elena had shot him in the left shoulder and his arm was shattered and burned. But he was still alive. Unconscious, or faking it, but definitely breathing.

I turned back to Elena. Mandeep injected some kind of fluid into her arm. Elena's body convulsed. I turned away as bile rose in my throat.

Thatcher moaned. I stepped toward him, shaking with rage.

I wanted to kill him. I wanted to kill him so badly I could taste it. Suddenly I was on him, punching his face over and over.

Then a hand wrenched my shoulder, pulling me off him. I spun around, furious.

Fatima was holding her hands up. "Chris, whoa. Stop!" she said. "This isn't you."

I turned and punched Thatcher again until she grabbed me and held my arms tight.

"This isn't you and it won't help Elena."

I went still and she released me.

I spat. My knuckles hurt. I shook with impotent rage.

I stepped away and watched as Fatima bent down and tied Thatcher's feet back together.

Thatcher was alive because of me. Because killing him "wasn't me." Elena was hurt and possibly dying, because of me. I wanted to yell, scream, kick Thatcher's ribs until they cracked. But Fatima was right. That wasn't me. And it wouldn't help Elena. A wave of disgust, at myself, at everything, washed over me and I began to cry.

Then Fatima's voice broke through again. "Where's Pavel?"

We looked around. There was a trail of blood on the floor, Elena's or Thatcher's, leading back to the bathroom. I followed it.

Pavel was slumped up against the inside wall of the shower. The water was still on, streaming down over his head. His motionless head.

I ran over and began shaking him. "Pavel?"

He didn't say anything. A line of blood ran from his nose and joined the water as it went spiraling down the drain.

"PAVEL!"

The water slowed to a trickle and then stopped. It was on a three-minute timer. Whatever had happened had all happened in a span of just three minutes.

Pavel's head lolled to one side and rested on my shoulder. I hugged him and began to cry again. Great heaving sobs.

Suddenly there was a choking sound, and Pavel coughed up a mixture of water and blood. He trembled, and his eyes opened a crack.

"What happened?" I said.

"He was too fast," Pavel said. "He wasn't supposed to do that." He coughed and spat out a gob of reddish water. "I was leaning down to help him get dressed when he slammed his head into my face. Then he hit me with his knee . . . or something. I don't remember what happened next. He wasn't supposed . . ." His head lolled again.

"It's okay," I said, holding him steady.

Fatima came rushing up. "Chris, you should go see Elena."

"Is she okay?" I choked up.

"More than okay." She even gave me a quick smile. "That girl is a force of nature."

I felt a rush of relief and hurried back, wondering what "more than okay" meant. I saw in a second.

Elena had gotten to her feet and grabbed her blaster. She was screaming, "Let me go!"

Mandeep was struggling to hold Elena back. Thatcher

had slid across the floor and was slumped against the wall. His eyes were locked on Elena's blaster. He didn't look scared. He looked hungry for it.

"Elena," I said. "Stop."

"She's not listening," Mandeep said.

"He's too dangerous to keep alive," Elena said. "I have to kill him *now*."

"Look at him," I pointed at Thatcher. "He's not going anywhere. And he's not going to hurt anyone."

I walked in front of her and held my hands up to calm her down, a technique she hated. But I figured she wasn't going to shoot me, so I stood between her and Thatcher.

"Where's Pavel?" she said.

"Pavel is not dead," I said. "I just saw him. He's really hurt but he's not dead. Fatima is watching him."

Then Elena looked at me and said something I never expected. "Pavel set him free."

The words hit me like a blow to the chest. "What?"

"I saw him. They got in the shower, and then Pavel cut his hands free."

It seemed impossible, but I knew there was no way that Elena would lie about this. She continued.

"I tried to stop him, but then Thatcher slammed Pavel into my chest. Thatcher grabbed the knife and came at me. I tried to scramble up, to get a clear shot, but he slashed me with the knife and kicked me over. He was moving so fast I couldn't fire without risking a hit on the hull."

"So he ran away," I said.

Elena took a few steps to her right and glared past me at Thatcher. "I followed. He was heading for the bridge," she said, her teeth clenched. "He was going to kill all of you. Then I knew I had no choice. I shot."

There was a low, rasping noise from the wall—hoarse, like fingernails on a chalkboard. Thatcher was . . . laughing?

"You stupid grinder-loving fools. Ten minutes alone with that boy was all I needed to turn him against you." He laughed again, then fell into a coughing fit. "He knows you are doomed. I promised him I'd let you all live. Everyone but the filthy grinder."

"No. That's impossible," I said. But then I remembered Pavel's words. *He wasn't supposed to . . .*

"I just told him what you already know. There's no way you'll make it to Earth alive without me in charge. And there's no scenario where you survive after that, unless you set me free." He began laughing again, a scraping choke. "So he agreed to help me, to save himself."

I glared at Thatcher, incredulous. He looked wounded but triumphant.

Elena raised her blaster and pointed it at his chest. I didn't move as she wrapped her finger around the trigger. But she didn't fire.

"We have to kill him. Now. Chris, just give me the order."

I said nothing.

Thatcher looked down at his chest. "Go ahead. But kill me and you will never make it home. Pavel told me about the Oracle. You're in range, so I know you were dumb enough to answer."

I stared at the floor.

He laughed. "I knew it Nichols. You think my troops didn't pick that signal up? If they didn't know you were coming before, they know exactly where you are right now."

As if on cue, there was a squawk of static on the radio followed by a woman's voice.

"*Hailing Melming Mining transport* Medusa. *You are about to enter restricted space. In order to proceed, transmit proper security codes.*"

I sneered at Thatcher. "We don't need you anymore," I said.

"I'll believe that when I see it," he said.

"Just watch me."

I turned to Elena. "If he moves a muscle, shoot him."

Elena gave a short nod, keeping her eyes and blaster level, aimed right at Thatcher, her finger coiled and ready.

I walked into the bridge as the message repeated.

"Yeah, yeah. Hold your horses," I muttered. I sat down at the console and turned on the microphone. I tried to make my voice sound as deep as possible.

"MMS *Medusa*, over. Sending codes." I turned off the microphone and began typing in the numbers the Oracle had given me.

45. 91. 39. 10. 75. 22.

Then I sat back and waited, holding my breath.

After a few seconds, the voice returned. *"Codes not recognized. I repeat. You are unauthorized to enter security perimeter. Send proper codes now or we will take all necessary action."*

I carefully typed in the numbers again, making absolutely sure I'd gotten them right.

45. 91. 39. 10. 75. 22.

I felt a bead of sweat on my forehead. "I'm watching," Thatcher called hoarsely from the hall, chuckling and coughing.

"Shut up," Elena said.

Once again the woman's voice returned, dissatisfied. *"Codes not recognized. This is your final warning."*

Thatcher laughed.

I bent my head to my chest. We were trapped. Everything I'd tried had gone wrong. I'd responded to the Oracle—leading them to our coordinates—for a useless code. Maybe it had been another trap all along. Not the Oracle at all but a decoy, luring me to stupidly reveal our position by using our transmitter.

Thatcher had obviously timed his escape attempt to coincide with crossing the border into Earth's defensive zone. He'd outsmarted me again.

"MMS Medusa. *Ships are being dispatched. If you continue on course you will be intercepted and destroyed."*

"They'll be in firing range in about fifty minutes," Thatcher said.

"Elena," I called. "Bring him in."

"What?" She sounded shocked, furious. "Chris, no. It's some kind of trick!"

"It doesn't matter. We have no choice." I almost added, "It's over." But I just couldn't accept that . . . at least not yet.

Chapter Fifteen
Trajectory

Thatcher lurched in, his injured arm dangling at his side. Mandeep had taped his other arm to his body. I marveled again at his ability to accept incredible pain. He must have had his nervous system removed.

Elena nudged him forward with the muzzle of the blaster. "Mandeep has gone to help Fatima with Pavel. Our other prisoner."

I didn't respond. I activated the microphone.

"This is MMS *Medusa*. We have Thatcher. Repeat. We have Thatcher."

I looked over at Thatcher's face; a smug grin stared back. "Identify yourself," I said. "Tell them we have you prisoner."

I was taking yet another giant risk. I had no idea what he would say. He could tell them to go ahead and destroy us. He could tell some secret code that would trigger something in the ship like knock-out gas.

Or he could tell them not to attack and to let us pass.

"Confirm identity," the voice said.

"Jimenez. I recognize your voice. This is Major Kirk Thatcher. I am being held against my will."

"Understood."

"The codes are Echo-Miner-555-Delta. I repeat, Echo-Miner-555-Delta."

There was a long silence as Jimenez, whoever she was, checked this against her database. There was probably some kind of voice recognition software too, I realized. I felt utterly defeated. When she returned, she addressed me instead of Thatcher.

"MMS Medusa. *You will proceed on your current path. An escort drone will join you in orbit and direct you to Earth. You will make no attempt to deviate from the course they give you or you will be destroyed."*

I shot a look at Thatcher, who stared back at me, his eyes locked on mine. "I told you, Nichols. No escape."

"MMS Medusa. *We will require verbal notification from Major Thatcher every hour or you will be destroyed. Do you understand?"*

"Oh. They understand perfectly, Jimenez," Thatcher said. "Talk to you in an hour."

"Aye aye, sir. Over and out."

I flicked off the microphone and slammed back into my chair.

Elena gave a short, loud scream of frustration and smacked Thatcher in the back of the head. Thatcher jolted forward and slammed his forehead on the console. Then he slumped down to the ground.

"Are you nuts?" I said.

"We'll wake him up in an hour," Elena said.

"If he's alive!" I jumped over and checked his neck. His pulse was low but still there, thank goodness.

We lifted him back into the pilot's chair and used the last of Mandeep's tape to tie him in place.

Elena finally lowered her blaster.

"So," she said. "Now what do we do about Pavel?"

Chapter Sixteen
Orbit

The Earth filled the screen. Blue, round, gorgeous, and, despite my years on Perses, home. It seemed close enough to touch, and yet hopelessly far away. Doom waited for us there. Thatcher's troops, Melming Mining's troops, whatever you wanted to call them, were going to take us out before we'd even have a chance to expose them. We could try to use Thatcher as a hostage, escape, but would that really work against a mob of fully armed soldiers? I didn't think so.

We'd defeated the Landers on Perses, but we'd had diggers, blasters, the element of surprise, and a huge bomb. It had been on our turf.

None of us had stepped on Earth in years. How much had it changed?

My mind raced for a solution and came up with nothing.

The speaker came to life.

"MMS Medusa, *prepare for an escort to dock in ten, nine, eight, seven . . ."*

The bridge door opened behind me. Droplets of water hit the floor.

"Bring him in," I said, without turning around.

Thatcher appeared, smelling like something between a wet dog and a urinal.

Between the hourly updates, we were now keeping him in the shower stall, tied to Pavel. Their hands and feet were bound with makeshift ropes made from torn sheets.

"If they want to pee their pants, they can clean themselves," Elena had said bitterly. They were stripped down to their underwear, just in case Pavel had tried to hide any more knives. Every once in a while we'd hear the water turn on and off.

Mandeep had done her best to patch them up and volunteered to keep watch. Pavel mostly avoided eye contact, his big mouth taped shut. We kept Thatcher's mouth taped as well . . . except for the hourly updates his troops demanded.

"... *three, two, one.*" There was a loud *clunk* as the escort rocket latched onto our hull. The console lit up as their guidance system took over control of our ship. Now we were just a tin can being led against our will. We slowly leveled out, the spinning no longer necessary as we were pulled more and more by Earth's gravity. I felt a mixture of relief and fear. I'd been worried about landing the ship, despite Elena's overwhelming confidence she could do it. Now a robot would guide us safely to the surface . . . where we faced almost certain death.

Thatcher was now sitting in the pilot's chair, his hands still tied together, his hair matted with filth. I flicked on our microphone.

"Link success," Thatcher said. "See you at HQ. Over."

"We'll be ready," Jimenez, or some other flunky, said.

"And make sure no one at Melming knows about this. Over."

"Yes, sir. Over and out."

Thatcher turned to me. "You're lucky that Rosales didn't kill me. You'd be getting blasted out of the sky right now instead of getting a nice lift home."

"Shut up," I said.

"Of course, you'll still die after we land. But at least you got to enjoy a few extra days of my company, and a final look at Earth." He nodded toward the window and laughed.

Fatima came up behind him and roughly slapped a thin piece of tape over his mouth. Thatcher's smile didn't vanish. He kept his eyes locked on mine, defiant, triumphant. Fatima and Elena grabbed him by the shoulders to lead him back to the shower.

"Wait," I said. "Leave him here. They might want to check in on him more often now that we're docked. To make sure he's alive."

"Seriously?"

"Just do it," I said sharply.

Elena shoved Thatcher back down into the chair. He grimaced briefly, then settled in, his eyes following me as I got up and marched off the bridge. What I actually wanted was to talk to Pavel one last time, alone.

I stepped through the door and into the bathroom. Mandeep looked up sleepily. "Go get some rest," I said.

Without saying anything, she yawned, got up, and walked past me, closing the door. Pavel lay hunched against the wall of the shower, sleeping. He smelled like a sewer.

I crouched down and ripped the tape off his face. He jerked awake, his eyes wide with panic. "What? Who . . ."

Then he saw me and slumped back into the stall. "Oh. What do you want?"

"I want to know why. Why did you help him after all we've been through?"

Pavel looked away. "Because he's right. We're doomed."

I took a deep breath. "That doesn't explain why you set him free. Why you helped him."

"You saw the way Fatima and Elena looked at him. They'd have killed him eventually, whether you let them or not. Then *we'd* be killed. You should be thanking me."

"You're lucky I don't throw you out the airlock," I said, then I forced myself to calm down. "He's going to kill us anyway," I added more quietly.

"He says he won't. At least not me."

I just shook my head. I remembered how Thatcher had tried to convince me to betray my friends when I'd been his prisoner. I hadn't bought the arguments. Pavel clearly had.

"He promised he'd let us all live, as long as he could kill the grinder." Pavel's voice trailed off.

"She has a name."

Pavel scoffed.

"And what was the first thing he did? Knocked *you* into the wall and tried to kill *you*."

Pavel gave a snort. "Nice try. He did that because stupid Elena looked like she was going to shoot him."

Thatcher was a master at getting people to believe his lies. Pavel's stubborn distrust of grinders combined with his cowardice had just made him an easier mark. But I had something more important I needed to find out—just how deeply had he betrayed us? I put my hand under his chin and lifted his head until our eyes met.

"Pavel. Did you tell him about the video?"

Pavel flinched and fought to look away.

"The video of Thatcher killing Nazeem. Did you tell him?"

Pavel's lips trembled. I didn't need to hear the words anymore. He looked as guilty as a kid who's stolen a chocolate bar from his mother.

I let go of his chin.

"He doesn't know what it is," Pavel said hurriedly. "I just told him that there was a video on the ship computer that could help the grinders."

"The ship computer?"

Pavel nodded quickly. "Just the one. The copy. He doesn't know about the original."

I stood up. Disgusted. Furious. Thatcher would erase the copy the first chance he got.

But Pavel hadn't totally screwed up, not yet.

Thatcher didn't know about the original, the video that was stored on the digger in the cargo bay. It was the faintest glimmer of hope. If there was some way to broadcast that before the troops took us prisoner, or worse . . . The problem was that the person who could tell me how to do that was sitting in front of me, brainwashed by Thatcher.

"Are you going to kill me?" Pavel whimpered.

I peeled off a fresh strip of tape and then bent down to place it over his mouth. He struggled, his eyes flashing. But the tape held. I turned and walked away.

Pavel had felt our plan, my plan, was hopeless. Thatcher had exploited that. He was an expert at it. But there was still a chance. I just didn't know exactly what it was.

For now, I knew one thing. Pavel and Thatcher couldn't be allowed in the same room together again.

Chapter Seventeen

Re-entry

Streaks of super-heated gas licked the hull as we began our descent toward Earth.

Thatcher was tied up in the pilot's seat to my right. Mandeep had hit him with a large dose of muscle relaxant she'd found in the ship's stores. He was asleep or at least unconscious.

Fatima and Elena were behind us, strapped into the other bridge chairs.

Elena had been largely silent ever since we'd been grabbed by the escort rocket. We'd had a few furtive conversations about what we could do next, but they hadn't gotten us anywhere concrete. She seemed just as depressed as I was.

Fatima, on the other hand, had grown more combative. "I'm going to be the first one they kill. And I'm not going down without a fight."

"I'm pretty sure we're going to get one," I said.

Elena tapped the side of her blaster. "If things look really bleak, I say we shoot Thatcher before they shoot us. At least this trip will have achieved one good thing."

I nodded, not in agreement, but in resignation. There were only a few ways this could go down once we landed, and none of them were good. We could somehow use Thatcher as a hostage or shield to secure our own release. But that didn't seem likely. There would be dozens of armed troops waiting for us on the ground.

A shoot-out would end up with all of us dead, even if we took out Thatcher and a few of his troops.

"*MMS* Medusa, *prepare to enter the atmosphere.*"

The blast shields on the windows lowered, blocking out the view of Earth's oceans, its clouds, its green. It all seemed so peaceful.

I had tried to broadcast from the bridge, send a distress signal, but the escort was jamming all our communications. I'd searched for the video file of Nazeem's death, but either I couldn't find it or it was gone.

There was still the digger in the cargo hold, with the original video. But once we were dead, it wouldn't take Thatcher long to discover that and have it erased.

The bridge began to shake. My teeth rattled as Earth's gravity gained an iron grip on us. Thatcher's head was pressed back in his seat, his eyes shut.

I had taped Darcy's birthday card back onto the console. It had been there when we left Perses. I wanted it to be the last thing I saw as we headed toward certain death.

The cake and candles shook violently, the candlelight seeming to flicker. I gazed at it, forgetting our situation, and it lulled me, calmed me.

And my brain woke up.

Escort ship. Video. Digger. I did my best to fight the g-force and turned to catch Elena's eye. She saw me turn and raised an eyebrow.

I raised mine back and smiled, not wanting to risk saying anything in front of Thatcher.

Elena cocked her head but smiled back. She knew I had some kind of plan, or the beginning of one. But now I needed a lot of things to work out in exactly the right way. And that had me worried. Because nothing had worked out that way so far.

We spent the rest of the trip in relative silence. From

time to time a voice would come over the speakers informing us of the stages of re-entry. With each second, my body seemed to drag and grow heavier.

Then, after what seemed like hours of shaking and rattling teeth, we began to slow. The escort ship had fired our forward blaster and we leveled out. The blast screens raised and the bridge was flooded with light. The sky was so blue it seemed impossible. Fluffy clouds dotted the expanse like balls of suspended cotton. Their fringes were just beginning to turn a pale pink. Evening was falling. On Earth.

Despite my fear, I felt a swell of emotion. I hadn't set foot on the Earth in years, and yet it did still feel like home.

There was a clunk as our landing gear engaged, and the loud hiss of our landing thrusters firing at full blast.

Then a cloud of steam, smoke, and dust enveloped us. We were back on Earth.

I had to struggle to hold my head upright after so long in space, but as I gazed straight ahead, I saw more than thirty figures, all dressed in black, emerge from the fog. Their blasters raised in front of them.

I reached out and tried to grab Darcy's card. The effort of raising my arms was too much. My fingers, unaccustomed to the gravity of Earth, fumbled. The card fell to the floor.

The troops moved closer.

I unbuckled myself and started counting down the seconds we had left before they reached us.

Chapter Eighteen

Grind

We needed to move, fast, if my plan had any hope. That was a problem because my legs felt like they were made of lead. I struggled to lift my feet even a fraction of an inch. It was like trying to walk through a giant pit of mud. My lungs heaved with the effort of breathing in the thick, heavy air.

The troops marched slowly, cautiously, but ever closer.

I reached down for Darcy's card and fell. I grabbed it, my fumbling fingers crumpling the paper. I tried to stand again, but I could barely get to my knees.

Someone grabbed my arm and I looked up. "Potato sack races," Elena said, standing, her other arm gripping her seat belt like a rope. "Just like in school."

I tucked the card in my pocket and we slung our arms around each other's shoulders and began walking in tandem.

Fatima had unbuckled herself and was leaning on the arms of her chair, pushing herself to get up. We shuffled over. Elena leaned down, and Fatima grabbed her forearm and pulled herself upright.

"Let's get Mandeep," I said. She and Pavel had been strapped into the seats in the dining room.

"What about him?" Fatima said, jerking her head slowly toward Thatcher. I hesitated, unsure of what we should, or could, do with him. I hadn't expected to feel so incredibly groggy, defenseless.

The speaker crackled to life. *"MMS* Medusa. *Prepare to be boarded. One false move and we will open fire. The doors will open in one minute."*

There was a hiss as the cabin began to slowly introduce outside air into the ship.

Elena pulled her shirt over her mouth. "Probably some kind of knockout gas mixed in with that."

"Gas masks," I said. Fatima pulled hers out from the compartment under her seat. She seemed to be moving in a kind of slow motion, but she slung it across her face. Then she grabbed two more and handed them to us.

Thatcher was awake now, struggling to free him-self, yelling something that was muffled by the tape on his mouth. His teeth gnashed against the tape, cutting holes in it.

If he got through it before he was knocked out, he'd warn them that we were up to something, even if he didn't know what.

"Leave him," I said.

"I will," Elena said. She raised her blaster and aimed it at the back of his head. Before she could pull the trig-ger, the entire transport was rocked by an explosion. The ship listed and began sliding sideways. We lost our footing and fell. Elena's arm struck the side of Fatima's chair, and the blaster was knocked loose. It skidded across the floor and slammed against the wall, then starting making a horrible high-pitched squeal.

"We need to go!" I said.

Our boots slid as we struggled to gain any kind of grip on the now-sloped floor.

"Crawl!" Elena said. We used everything we could grab as a handhold, pulling ourselves away from Thatcher, the overheating blaster, and whatever was going on outside.

"Why would they be firing at us with Thatcher still in here?" Fatima asked.

I craned my neck to steal a peek back out the bridge window. "It's not his troops!" The shooting was coming from the mist behind them. More blaster traces burned a path toward the troops, making wisps as they found their marks. More and more soldiers fell. Another huge blast hit the ground outside, shaking the transport and sending clumps of mud onto the window.

Some of Thatcher's troops turned and began sprinting toward the attackers, firing repeatedly.

"Grinders," Fatima said excitedly. "They're here! I knew it!"

"Let's hurry!"

Thatcher continued to thrash in his seat, then he made a loud spitting sound, and I knew he'd chewed through the tape. "They are running! Fire on the mid-cabin, you idiots!"

There was a loud boom and the transport shook violently. Another boom and it began to list even more to the side.

"Again!" he yelled.

We got to our feet and opened the bridge door. Red emergency lights flashed and a siren wailed.

Mandeep was on her knees, struggling to put an oxygen mask on Pavel, who lay on the floor. She was already wearing hers. Fatima walked over, finding her feet more securely, and grabbed the mask.

"He won't need it," she yelled. "But we will."

Mandeep looked confused. "But he's hurt. He unbuckled himself somehow but hit his head or something. He's out cold. I can't wake him."

"Let's go," I said. Those were two of the hardest words I'd ever spoken. We couldn't risk carrying him if we were going to escape. We could barely move ourselves.

"Go? Where?"

I looked at Pavel before risking an answer. "Just come with us."

Mandeep looked from Pavel to me and back again. "But . . ."

Another blast rocked the ship.

"No time to debate," Elena said.

Mandeep took Elena's hand, her eyes on Pavel.

We continued shuffling forward, now crouching awkwardly. Smoke billowed around us. Holes and cracks began showing in the thick metal. We gained our footing with each step. When we reached the cargo hold, the door slid open with a slight hiss of air.

The digger sat, perfectly still, held in place by large steel cables.

"So now that we're free of Thatcher and the spy, what's the plan?" Elena asked.

"Assuming you actually have one," Fatima said.

"Up ahead," I said, pointing to the digger. "We do what we do best. Run. Hide. Survive."

We repeated the phrase together. "Run. Hide. Survive."

More blasts hit the side of the ship.

Elena, Mandeep, and Fatima began unhitching the hooks that held the cables to the floor.

I opened the cockpit lid and slipped into the driver's seat. Elena was our best driver, but I wanted to be sure of only one more thing before we left. I turned on the power and the dashboard lit up.

I flicked a switch and the screen was filled with the video. Our last hope of showing the world the truth. The image showed Nazeem lying on the floor, helpless and dying. Thatcher raised his blaster. I couldn't bear to watch anymore. I turned it off, but I also breathed a sigh of relief.

I flicked on the ignition and the digger roared to life.

Elena's head popped up. "Move over," she said, and climbed in, setting herself up behind the steering column.

"This is going to be tight," Fatima said, sitting down next to her. I shuffled over and pressed myself against the side. Mandeep undid the final hook and got in, squeezing beside Fatima.

It was uncomfortable, our rear ends jammed up

against each other, Elena's hip bone jabbing into mine.

"Okay, MiNRs," Elena said, slapping the *M* tattoo on her arm. "Here we go."

She inched forward, waiting for the auto sensor to open the door. "We'll have to blast through at top speed and too bad for whoever is in front of us when we do."

The nose cone of the digger nudged the metal of the cargo bay door, but it stayed shut.

"The door isn't opening," Mandeep said, panic in her voice.

There was a manual override for everything on this ship, and the one for the cargo door was close.

Without hesitating, I opened the cockpit lid and leaped out. There was a metal box next to the doorway. Inside was a red handle, like a large light switch. I flicked it upward and it clicked into position. A flashing light started whirling overheard as the door began to open. Light and smoke poured in from the growing gap on the floor.

"Hurry!" Elena called.

I ran back and was reaching for the side to pull myself in when the hallway door slid open. I froze. If Thatcher had recovered Elena's blaster, we were doomed.

But it was Pavel, limping and holding onto the wall for support.

"Wait," he said. "Don't leave me."

I turned just as a blast shook the ship. A giant chunk of metal smashed down, ripping a hole in the floor. A plume of fire shot out of the gap, just missing me and the digger.

"We're sitting ducks!" Mandeep yelled.

Elena looked over the edge. "Chris. NOW!"

I scrambled into the cockpit as Pavel fell forward, his body hitting the floor with a sickening thud.

Elena closed the lid and the cargo bay door opened just enough for us to pass underneath. She hit the power. We flew out the door at full speed into a scene of death and chaos.

Chapter Nineteen
Pointless

Black-uniformed soldiers jumped out of our way as we cut a path. Not all were fast enough. I closed my eyes but the image of Pavel's face filled the darkness. I immediately opened them again. A group of camouflaged fighters were firing into the air behind us. As we passed through, they began to fall back and retreat into the smoke and trees.

"Grinders!" Fatima cheered, banging her palms against the window in excitement.

"They're buying us some time," Elena said.

"Time for what?" Mandeep asked.

"Escape," I yelled over the roar of the digger.

"Damn right," Fatima said.

"Let's not waste it," Elena said. She fired up the disrupter and angled the nose toward the ground. Just before we dove down, I saw a strange sight. One of the grinders, a woman in dark overalls, waved at us. It seemed so out of place with the chaos surrounding her.

In a flash the deadly battle scene was replaced by a solid wall of dark rock and dirt.

The digger lurched and sputtered as we smashed into an underground sewer line. Elena put it in reverse and broke through the other side. But moments later we hit a pocket of underground power lines, the nose cone cutting quickly through their housing. Sparks and flashes of electric blue zapped up and down the sides of the digger like lightning. The digger froze.

Elena waited a second, then hit reverse again.

"Earth sucks," she said.

"There's too much stuff here to dig," Fatima said.

"They're coming after us!" Mandeep's eyes darted around as if she expected Thatcher and his troops to appear at any moment.

"Go deeper!" I said. "Just head straight down from here. We'll hit some kind of bedrock eventually."

Elena jammed the nose cone straight down and began digging more carefully. We hit more holes, but we made progress.

Finally, we began digging through rock. I wasn't sure how far underground we were, but it was far.

Elena leveled us out and fired the disrupter again. Now we zoomed ahead burning a path away from Thatcher and his troops.

"Where are we?" Mandeep asked.

"About ten miles under the planet's crust," Elena said. "I think."

"No wonder it's so hot," I said. If Elena was right, we were about halfway between the surface and the molten mantle. The map on the screen was useless, set for Perses and seemingly unable to determine that we were on Earth. At least the internal compass could determine magnetic north, so we knew which direction we were facing. West.

"Where did we even land?" Fatima asked. "I mean, we could be heading for a cliff or straight into the ocean."

Elena slowed down. "Good point," she said. She turned to me. "Fearless?"

"I know, I know. 'What do we do now?'"

They stared at me.

The problem was, I had no idea.

"I had an escape plan," I said. "That worked."

"Thanks to the grinders," Fatima said, practically beaming.

"No kidding," I agreed. "Now we need to figure out a way to keep on the move without being tracked. And we need to get that video to someone we can trust."

"And we need to find some food and water," Mandeep said. "We left everything back on the transport."

"Including Pavel," I said sadly. I'd made the right decision to leave him, but the look on his face as he begged me to save him . . . it haunted me.

Mandeep didn't say anything but Fatima shook her head. "He made his bargain. And he almost got us all killed."

"If you'd run back to get him, we'd all be dead," Mandeep said.

Shouldn't I have tried? I wondered, but only to myself.

Elena slowed the digger to a crawl, then stopped.

"Pavel couldn't be trusted," she said, taking my hand in hers. "You know that. If we'd brought him with us, we'd have to watch him. Keep him from the computer. Keep him from the digger. That's no way to avoid being tracked."

I sighed. "You didn't see his face. He was scared."

"He should be," Fatima said.

I hung my head. Despite everything he'd done, he was one of us. But like Jimmi, he'd chosen to save himself. He'd fallen for the same lies as who knew how many people on Earth. I could only hope that Thatcher and his troops would show some mercy. Or maybe the grinders won the battle and they'd save him. Given his persistent hatred of grinders, it would be a fitting irony. Exhaustion hit me like a punch. Despite my racing mind, I yawned.

"I haven't slept in days," I said.

"Good call," Elena said. "I'll take first watch, and we'll proceed slowly. We'll also need to figure out a way to recharge the battery. And how to cover our tracks."

The gentle rocking of the digger eventually drowned out the noise in my mind and I drifted into a deep sleep.

Chapter Twenty
Digits

Numbers came flooding out of the digger console at me, armed like soldiers, their blasters pointed at my head. The lead one turned into Pavel, his face twisted with an evil smirk. He yelled, "Fire!"

I stared at the screen in a panic, a cold sweat running down my back. It took a few seconds to realize that I was awake.

Fatima was now driving the digger while Elena and Mandeep slept, resting against each other's shoulders.

"Good sleep?" Fatima whispered.

"Ugh." The numbers were still swimming in front of my eyes, almost like they were alive. "I hate that groggy feeling when you wake up from a nap."

"Nap?" she chuckled. "You've been crashed for hours."

I sat up straighter, wiping my hand over my face to erase the cobwebs.

"What was your dream about?"

"Numbers."

"Numbers?" She smirked. "Elena's right. You are a math geek."

"These ones were real."

"Real? Why? What numbers were they?" she asked.

I closed my eyes. "The landing code the Oracle had sent us."

"The one that didn't work," Fatima said.

I nodded. "No wonder they were trying to kill me in my dream."

"I bet the Melming thugs listened in on the transmission, then changed them."

"Maybe." I stared silently out at the disintegrating rock for a few minutes. "I wonder how the grinders knew where we were going to land?"

"Could be that they were listening in too. Or maybe the Oracle is working with them. She knew somehow and tipped them off."

"Hmm," I said. "Thatcher did say something about meeting Jimenez at HQ. I assumed he meant Melming Mining HQ."

"In Oslo."

"Yeah. But that didn't look like Oslo. There were palm trees."

Truth was, with the console basically shut down during the landing, I really had little idea where we'd ended up.

"So Thatcher and his troops have their own base of operations," Fatima said.

"Maybe on a secret island somewhere," I said.

"He probably has his own swivel chair in his office, like all the evil guys from old movies."

"With an evil-looking cat perched on his lap."

"Licking its lips as it imagines munching on us like giant mice."

I chuckled at the image. Too loudly. Elena and Mandeep opened their eyes and stretched.

"We miss something funny?" Elena asked, stretching her arms.

"No," I said. "Just letting off some steam."

"I need to go to the bathroom," Mandeep said.

"On it," Fatima said. She turned the digger sharply to the right and dug into the rock about twenty feet. Then she turned, dug a hole down a foot, turned off the disrupter and backed up all the way into the tunnel. "There ya go. A nice little bathroom, custom-made for privacy."

Mandeep hopped out and disappeared around the curve. As I waited my turn, I wondered about what we could possibly do now. I wasn't the only one.

"We've got to go up to the surface and see where the heck we are," Elena said. "Otherwise we'll run out of oxygen, power, patience."

"What if we're caught? They must be looking everywhere for us," Fatima said.

"Maybe not," I said.

"Meaning?"

"Thatcher doesn't want everyone knowing he's trying to kill off a bunch of kids. He'll be tracking us, but as quietly as possible."

"Maybe we should blow that up by going public," said Fatima.

"Risky," Elena said. "The Oracle warned us about how many people support, and believe, Thatcher. We could surface in the middle of some scary places."

"Agreed," I said. "If we knew we'd find someone we could trust, it would be worth the risk. But I bet there are plenty of Thatcher lovers up there just itching to turn over a bunch of grinder rebels to the authorities. Remember, he's spent years scapegoating grinders."

"Maybe these tattoos were a stupid idea after all," Fatima said.

"No," Elena said, flexing her shoulder muscle and tapping the *M*. "We stick together. Grinder and miner. That's what this tattoo represents. If it means they kill us together, so be it."

She held out her hand and Fatima took it firmly, giving Elena a punch on her tattoo. Elena grinned and returned the gesture.

"But eventually, we'll have to find someone we can trust," Fatima said. "We can't run forever."

Mandeep walked back toward us. "Why not just broadcast the video all over the place? 'A picture is worth a thousand words.' Right?"

"That's true," I said. "And I'd hoped the Oracle could do that. She has a transmitter. But who knows if she's even alive."

"Does anyone here know anyone on Earth they can trust?"

We looked around. No one answered.

"Anyway, my turn," Elena said. She jumped out of the digger and walked down the tunnel. "I expect you to have this all solved before I get back."

"What were the numbers the Oracle gave you?" Mandeep asked.

"45. 91. 39. 10. 75. 22. Maybe it's another grinder code?" My father and mother had used grinder codes to send us messages. And we'd used them to trick Thatcher into a trap back on Perses.

Fatima repeated the numbers out loud. "Maybe. But you always need a key code to know which number starts. Did she say anything else?"

I shook my head.

A loud rumble rolled down from the tunnel.

"We've been followed!" Mandeep said.

Fatima closed her eyes and strained to listen. "Not diggers!"

There was a giant *crack* followed by what sounded like thunder.

Fatima's eyes grew wide. "Cave-in!" she yelled. She closed the lid just as a crack split the ceiling down the middle.

A chunk of rock banged off the back of the digger as Fatima swerved into the wall and then turned sharply. "Faster inside the rock than in the tunnel," she said, grimacing as she struggled to keep the wheel in place.

"Elena!" I said.

"We're going to get her," Fatima said, teeth clenched.

We blasted through the wall and into the side tunnel Fatima had dug.

The place where Elena had been.

It was now completely filled with shattered stone.

Chapter Twenty-One
All Hands

I was out of the cockpit before Fatima could say anything, digging and clawing at the wall of rock. Small stones continued to fall from the ceiling, pinging off the rocks and my back.

"Elena!" I shouted. "Elena!!!"

"Chris, that won't work!" Fatima called. "There's too much."

"We can't use the digger," I said, without turning around. "It'll blow!"

Fatima and Mandeep jumped out and began digging next to me.

"This is a seriously dumb idea," Fatima said. "Cave-ins don't just stop."

But we kept grabbing stones and throwing them aside. I grabbed rock after rock and then . . . Elena's boot. Crushed under a pile of rubble. "Oh no," I said. "No. No. NO." I fell to my knees and reached for the boot, grabbing it from the pile. It came loose. Where was Elena's leg?

"What are you guys doing?" It was Elena's voice, but it was coming from behind us. She ran up and then stopped, hands resting on her knees, huffing and puffing. "There is not a lot of oxygen down here."

I stared at her like I was seeing a ghost.

"You weren't trapped!" I said, holding up the boot.

"How stupid do you think I am? Fatima's not the only one who knows what a cave-in feels like. You guys took off into the wall just as I bolted back into the tunnel. So I followed you. Nice to see you were coming back to get me." She smiled.

Elena grabbed the boot, then got down on the ground and slid it back on.

"Thanks. It's not easy running after a digger with only one boot."

There was a low rumble from the other side of the pile. "We gotta go," Fatima said.

We piled back into the digger—Elena back in the driver's seat.

I couldn't stop staring at Elena. She saw me and turned and smiled. "Don't worry so much, Fearless. I'm a soldier. I don't plan on dying in the latrine."

"I worry about everything," I said.

"No kidding," Mandeep and Fatima said at the same time.

I did worry about everything. But there was more than that. The thought of a world without Elena, even that brief glimpse, had gutted me.

Elena chuckled, then she turned her attention back to the dashboard. "Still heading west. But *whoa*. Batteries are seriously low. We've got no choice. We have to surface soon."

Elena began to angle the digger up, slowing. "Don't have any idea what's up ahead. And I don't want to hit it at top speed."

As we climbed, so did my anxiety.

No matter where we surfaced, there would be people. Possibly people who were friendly. Very likely people who were not. There would be security cameras, people with phone cameras, computers . . .

Even if we did get lucky and show up in some vacant lot or isolated field, where would we find power? Food?

Every good possibility seemed to be accompanied by an equally bad one.

All along the way I'd tried to make good decisions, but the fact was that we'd started out with more than a dozen survivors. Now there were four. I couldn't bear to think about Pavel, or Therese and Darcy back on Perses.

"How long have we been on the run?" I asked, more to distract myself than because I cared.

Fatima peeked at the clock. "Seven hours, fifteen minutes, and . . . thirty seconds."

"So it's probably the middle of the night wherever we are," I said. "That's one good thing, I suppose. Darkness."

We lapsed back into silence for a minute. The digger continued to rumble through the Earth toward . . . who knew?

"Every second we're not Thatcher's prisoners, we're winning," Elena said. "It means we've still got a chance to do something."

"I wonder what he's doing now," Fatima asked.

"Getting treated for a hundred injuries," I said. "It's not natural how much punishment that guy can take."

"He still bled when I smashed him in the arm with that blaster shot," Elena said. "So he's not a robot."

"Maybe he's some kind of genetic freak."

"He can bounce back quickly. Pretty good skill for a soldier in the field," Elena said.

I held up my hand and stared at the missing fingers in the pale light of the dashboard. I thought of my own surprising ability to recover. "Remember all those shots they gave us when we left for Perses?"

"At least a dozen," Elena said. "You think maybe we have some special powers?"

"Possibly," I said. "You got practically blown up by a bomb."

"With the scars to prove it," Elena said bitterly.

"My mom was part of the medical team," Mandeep said. "She called it the inoculation program—to protect us against diseases that might be on Perses. But maybe there was more."

"Meaning?" Fatima said.

"They knew we'd have to be strong to survive on a strange planet, so they gave everyone some kind of immune system booster shot?"

"And now maybe it's backfired against them," Fatima said. "Because we're tough."

"I like that thought," Elena said. She flexed her bicep.

"Maybe Thatcher knew about those boosters," I said. "Or found out about them once he got more into the Melming power structure."

"And figured our families weren't just normal people sent to live in space," Elena said.

"But could become dangerous, powerful potential enemies."

"So he took us out."

"Or tried to," Mandeep said.

We continued on in silence for a while. It was probably just a fantasy, but the more I thought about it, the more sense it made. This whole mission had been part of a grand experiment. Not just an experiment about mining in space, but an experiment about how well humans could survive, and thrive, *alone* in space. A scientific test of the limits of what humans could do.

Every time we learned something about the mission, we uncovered another layer of subterfuge and machination. It was like we were always . . .

"Mining," I chuckled.

"What?" Elena said.

"Nothing. Just a bad joke."

"How unlike you." Elena slugged me in the shoulder.

The digger jolted as we broke through into some kind of concrete tunnel. The disrupter immediately turned off, but the tracks continued to run.

Instead of driving through the other side, Elena stopped and turned off the power.

"What are you doing?" Mandeep said.

"Shhh." She opened the cockpit lid. The smell of raw

sewage burned my nose. I gagged. The trickle of running water echoed off the curved walls.

"At the least the air is cooler here," Fatima said, covering her mouth with her shirt.

Elena got up on the hood of the digger. "Sewers are near the surface. And they need access points for the gases to escape." The sun had long set but a light shone down, illuminating the dusty air in silver lines. It came from a grate just above us to the right. Elena tiptoed across the hull and peered up through the holes.

"Full moon," she said.

Mandeep ran her fingers through the light. "I'd forgotten how beautiful the moon was!"

"Not great for staying invisible," Fatima said.

She was right.

Elena turned toward us. "But the moon seems to be the only light. No streetlights or anything else like that."

"So we're close enough to civilization to have a sewer . . ." Mandeep said.

". . . but far enough away that there aren't a lot of people," Fatima finished.

"I'm going up," Elena said. "Boost me."

Fatima was closest, so she wrapped her arms around Elena's knees and lifted.

"Got it," Elena said, pushing the grate to the side as

quietly as she could. I helped Fatima steady herself as Elena stepped on her shoulders and grabbed the sides of the opening.

She pulled herself up and out, and disappeared.

There were a few tense seconds until Elena's face popped back into view. "All clear. Let's have a look around." She reached down and held out her arm.

Fatima climbed up.

"I'll stay with the digger," Mandeep said.

"Any sign of danger, you get the heck out of here," I said.

She nodded. Then she helped boost me, and I joined Elena and Fatima on top.

I brushed myself off and took in the surroundings. The moon was bright and beautiful. And the light clearly revealed that we were on a road, not far from a big expanse of water. Possibly a lake. Possibly the ocean. A warm breeze came in off the water. I licked the air. Salt. Definitely an ocean or sea. The waves lapped at a rocky shoreline. We slid the grate back in place and walked toward the water.

"Good thing we hit the sewer," Elena said. She pointed at the waves. "We could have ended up in that. And I don't want to find out how watertight our digger is."

We passed through a strip of tall grass, went down

a slope, and climbed on top of a giant boulder. Waves splashed against the rock face, sending dots of moonlit foam and salt onto our feet.

"So where are we?" Fatima asked. "It smells . . . feels . . . familiar." There was something odd in her voice, like she was distracted.

Elena turned to me. "Any ideas, space geek?" she asked.

I looked up at the constellations and couldn't help but smile as I scanned the millions of twinkling lights for patterns.

"Orion is visible, and the North Star. That obviously means we're in the northern hemisphere."

"Thanks, professor," Elena said. "You sound just like your mom."

"I'll take that as a compliment."

"You should," she said quietly.

It took me a while to find my bearings. I'd grown so used to the skies on Perses. But a childhood of star-gazing with my mom and dad came flooding back. I pointed to a group of seven bright stars.

"That's the Big Dipper," I said. "And those stars over there are Cassiopeia. Sailors could tell what direction they were heading just by knowing the location of those two."

"Just like those explorers you used to always go on about."

I sighed deeply. That felt like a different Christopher. "Yeah. But they had sextants and other instruments."

"So we're screwed?" Fatima said.

I held my arm straight out toward the horizon and made a fist, resting the side of my palm on the line of the water. "Nope. I've got my eyes. And my brain."

Elena and Fatima snorted.

I looked down my arm and estimated how far the North Star was from my hand.

"What are you doing?" Fatima asked.

"It's an old-fashioned way to determine latitude." I nodded toward my hand. "Because of the distance between my eyes and arm, the angle of my hand—when I look down my arm—is about ten degrees above the horizon. Like a triangle. My arm is the bottom side. My line of vision is the top." I ticked my head up and looked toward the sky. "The North Star is sitting about ten degrees above that."

"And?"

I lowered my arm. "It means we are farther north than you'd think."

"I didn't think we were anywhere," Elena said.

Fatima waved her off. "So what does that tell us?"

"We're somewhere on the coast of Portugal."

"Seriously? How do you know THAT?" Elena asked.

"The stars," I said, pointing. "And that sign over there in Portuguese."

The moonlight shone on a faded wooden sign with the words "Praia de São Jo . . ." written in blue. The last word had been blasted off by years of salty winds.

"That's Portuguese, isn't it?"

Elena rolled her eyes. "This guy's a real genius, eh Fatima?"

Fatima stared at the sign in silence. "You okay?" Elena and I said together.

Fatima looked away, the moonlight illuminating a line of moisture around her eyes. "Um. Fine." She gave a short cough, as if she couldn't quite talk yet.

In the short time we'd known each other, I hadn't seen Fatima show anything but steely resolution.

Elena put her hand on Fatima's shoulder. "Carvalho. That's a Portuguese name, right?"

"This is where you're from?" I asked.

Fatima nodded. "I was born here. My mother died when I was young. I remember my father taking me to see the ocean as a 'treat.' There was a boat. The man paid my father and took me away."

She spat onto the ground. "The smell is what I remember."

Elena hugged Fatima's shoulders, but Fatima's tears had dried in the wind.

"I never wanted to come back here," she said. "It seems like a bad omen that this is where we ended up surfacing."

"I don't believe in bad omens," Elena said. "I believe in us. And if we happen to run into your father or the jerk who owned the boat, we'll give them a proper thanks."

Fatima smiled.

"We should move," I said. "There must be towns near here with some supplies."

"But we should also try to set up a solar charger somewhere hidden to make sure we don't run out underground," Fatima said. "We'll have to be discreet. I'm sure there are people out there looking for us."

I nodded. Then I held my hand back up to the sky and watched the stars. I knew where we were, sort of. I still had no idea where we were headed.

Chapter Twenty-Two
Power

A quick swim in the warm water was just what the doctor'd ordered. Literally. Before she would let us back in the digger, Mandeep demanded we all clean up.

"Your BO alone could lead them right to us," she said.

It felt good to joke. It also felt good to wash off the grime from months in space, the last two weeks with no shower. The waves seemed to wash more energy through my fatigued and bruised body.

"Okay, Fearless, time to get moving," Elena called from the shore. "Found one towel in the trunk. Has some grease on it, but it should work."

I walked out of the water and onto the beach wearing

only my underwear and feeling a bit sheepish. The towel appeared out of nowhere and smacked me in the face. "Nice shot," I said.

"And I had my eyes closed," she said. "The moonlight on your skinny body makes you look like a sick fish."

"It's not like I've had a chance to get a tan." I used the tip of the towel to swab some water out of my ears. As the water dried, the salt made everything feel sticky, but I didn't care. I felt cleaner than I had in ages.

Elena was just pulling on her uniform and I caught a view of her out of the corner of my eye. I turned away quickly, blushing.

"Not sure we've got any secrets from each other anymore," Elena said, walking closer. I could see her smile in the moonlight.

"It's not even that . . . It's more . . ." I wondered if the moonlight was bright enough to show how red my cheeks were getting.

She took my hand. "I wish we could go back to that slow dance at the party," she said. "That was nice."

A lump rose in my throat. "Yeah."

She laced her fingers in mine and we stood there silently for a few seconds. Then she took her hand away. "What could have been, huh?" She stared down at her bare feet.

"Yeah," I said, trying not to look her in the eye. She walked away and I zipped up my uniform and followed.

Fatima's head popped out of the hole as we approached. She and Mandeep had taken the first baths, and her hair was still damp. "Sun's coming up," she said. I turned. A thin line of orange danced off the distant waves.

"Time to hide," I said.

We climbed through the hole as the sky brightened, sliding the metal grate back into place.

"So where to?" Mandeep asked as Elena settled back behind the wheel.

"That way," Elena said, pointing in the direction the sewage was flowing from. "Where there are toilets, there are people."

My stomach rumbled. "And maybe there'll be a snack bar?"

Elena turned the digger into the sludge and we began driving slowly up the tunnel.

We drove for about thirty minutes, then slowed, moving as quietly as we could, ready to launch into the rock at a moment's notice. The battery levels were dangerously low.

The sky turned pink and then blue in the grates as we passed under them.

Shadows moved quickly overhead. "Trucks or cars," Elena said. "Going to work."

There was an even louder rumble. "Maybe tractor trailers too."

"Or troop carriers," Fatima said.

Our ears were attuned to every ting, rattle, or movement. We reached a junction of three large sewers. Most of the waste was running, and running regularly, from the opening to the right. The one straight ahead was trickling with waste. The one to the left was almost bone dry.

"Not a lot of people that way," Elena said. "So that's where we head to repower. But first I want to see where we are."

Elena slowed down and pulled underneath a large grate, then she turned off the power. When she opened the cockpit lid a crack, more sounds filtered down with the dust. People talking. Dogs barking. Honking horns. Life on planet Earth. It seemed so surreal—normal, yet fraught with danger.

"It's not like we can go up there unnoticed," I said. I indicated our cleaner (but still dirty) orange overalls and grimy shirts.

Elena nodded. "Just want to get a peek to see what we can come back for at night."

She pushed the cockpit lid open the rest of the way and stood on the hood of the digger. She held her head on an angle to glimpse as much of the outside world as she could. After about a minute, she got back down and slipped inside.

"Small fishing village," she said. "Lots of traffic. But it all seems pretty innocuous."

"How about clothes and food?"

"Didn't see any shops, but there are clotheslines . . . I think. It was kind of hard to tell from that angle. And there has to be food somewhere."

"So do we dig our way up tonight?" Mandeep asked.

"Once the sun goes down," I said.

"We've got to be as invisible as possible," Elena said. "So the digger stays underground." She turned the engine back on and began snaking down the tunnel to our left.

After about half an hour, the tunnel began to climb. It ended abruptly under a large iron grate that looked like the door of a jail cell. Dead moss, sticks, and some plastic junk hung down from the bars. A rusty ladder ran from the floor to a smaller hinged opening. It must have been locked once, but the latch was empty now. A small break for us.

"Maybe it's a storm drain of some kind," Elena said.

"Doesn't look like it's rained much lately," Fatima said.

"Good," I said. "A nice sunny day is what we need."

"How long will it take to charge the digger?"

"I'm not a hundred percent sure," I said. "The charging stations back on Perses could do it in minutes. A small solar booster is going to take longer."

I hopped over the side of the digger and got the kit out of the trunk.

Elena had her ear cocked, listening for any sign of movement. "All clear," she said. She reached under the dashboard and popped the hood.

I attached the charging cords to the battery, then began climbing up the ladder. The bolts jiggled in the wall, sending pebbles of decayed concrete onto the hood.

"Be careful," Fatima said.

"Thanks. I hadn't thought of that," I joked. But I pressed more of my weight against the ladder to keep it from pulling away.

I reached the top and peered outside. Concrete ran away from the opening like the sides of a bowl. The grate was at the bottom.

"It's a storage pond of some kind," I called down. "Or a cistern or something."

"Is there enough sunlight to use that thing?" Elena asked.

I brushed aside some of the dead plants. The sun was directly overhead.

"I think so? We can at least get it started."

I pushed the small door open and pulled myself up. The entire area was surrounded by trees and shrubs. No humans or even animals that I could see. The far edges of the cistern were covered in thick moss. Grass was growing in large cracks everywhere. Whatever this place had been, it was now old and forgotten.

The solar panel kit was about the size of a book, but the panels were so thin that it actually covered an area as big as a king-sized bed once it was all unfolded and laid out on the ground.

I worried it might be too spread out, too visible, so I refolded some of the pieces back in and hoped that wouldn't affect the recharging capability too much.

Then I took a seat nearby, my eyes and ears alert for anything sinister, like the buzzing of a drone or the rumble of an approaching ship, tank, or troop carrier.

All I heard were birds singing in the distance. Seagulls flew overhead, squawking and soaring. It seemed so calm, so peaceful.

I took Darcy's card out of my pocket. It was now

crumpled, dirty, tearing at the edges. It looked like how I felt. I folded it back up, put it in my pocket, and stared at the sky.

Thatcher had access to surveillance satellites and must have been scanning everywhere. He knew we'd have to come up for air at some point.

I hoped the image of a kid hanging out in the middle of an old ruin wouldn't set off any alarms bells. Or maybe it would. I got up and made my way back to the ladder. I slipped inside and called down to Elena. She had her eyes glued to the dashboard.

"All good?"

She looked up at me. "Better than good. That thing works like a charm. We're already back up to twenty percent."

"Great!"

"Should only take another hour or so."

Fatima and Mandeep were laying out some blankets on the dry floor of the tunnel. It looked incredibly welcoming.

Mandeep threw Fatima another blanket. "Then we wait for night and head back to the town to do some shopping."

"Without being seen or heard," I said.

"Run silent and run deep," Elena said.

We all looked at her. "It's a bit of old military advice. For submarines. The best way to stay alive when ships were looking for you was to go as deep as possible and not make unnecessary noise."

"Sounds like a good plan."

Elena smiled a wicked smile. "But when the time comes, we make plenty of noise."

Chapter Twenty-Three
Shopping

Drip. Drip. Drip.

My eyes blinked open as small drops of water trickled down from above and landed on my face. There was a flash of lightning and a loud boom that echoed down the tunnel.

"Heck of an alarm clock," I said, wiping my hands over my face.

Elena was already up and folding her blanket into the back of the digger.

"Perfect cover, though."

"If you say so."

I wiped the sleep from my eyes and felt the clammy

dampness of my uniform sticking to my legs. I was soaked.

"C'mon, sleepyhead," Elena said. "If we hurry we can use the storm to hide any noise we make, and any tracks we leave behind."

She walked over and shook Mandeep, who looked just as groggy as I felt. Fatima was sitting up, rubbing her face with her hand. She shook her curly hair and water sprayed out like a fountain.

"I had a dog that used to do that," Mandeep said.

"Woof," Fatima said. "I'd settle for dog food right about now."

My stomach gurgled. "I'm starving too."

"Well, the food's thataway," Elena said, pointing her arm down into the darkness. "Who's with me?"

We quickly set off to the village.

The storm continued to rage above us. Yes, it hid us, but it could equally cover up other sounds, like a landing troop ship or a battle digger. Still, all I heard were the crashes of thunder and the splash of heavy rain on our hood every time we passed under a grate.

We pulled up to the village area slowly and stopped below a huge iron gutter.

"We should park the digger here," Elena said. "Then we sneak up and grab whatever we can."

Mandeep again offered to stay behind.

I took Darcy's card out of my pocket and tucked it in the dashboard compartment.

Then Elena, Fatima, and I climbed up, one by one, onto the street.

The storm was right above us, lightning crashing, the rain coming down in sheets.

"Welcome home," Fatima said, the water pouring down her face.

"This seem like a good idea?" I said

Elena slugged my shoulder. "Don't be such a baby." She marched through the puddles. I thought of Darcy's reaction to the first storm we'd seen back on Perses. It had been joy, splashing in puddles, then fear as the storm had grown closer. Who knew how many new storms she'd seen by now? How violent had they become?

Each flash illuminated a row of buildings. Cinderblock and glass. Shops, rather than homes. Elena had already reached the first one and was peering inside the front window.

"See any cameras?" she asked, still peering but waving her arms in the direction of the outside roof.

I didn't see anything but soaking-wet concrete and metal siding. The rain was flowing over the gutters. There was practically a river heading down the middle of the street.

"Nope," I said.

Fatima frowned. "Whatever's inside must not be worth much."

Elena pulled her face away from the window. "Maybe not to a normal person. But there's a whole pile of what we need inside." Then, with one swift jab of her elbow, she smashed the glass on the front door.

I instinctively cringed, expecting the high-pitched squeal of an alarm.

But there was nothing, just the rain.

"How did you know there wasn't an alarm?" I asked as she reached through the door and unlocked the handle.

"Didn't. Just didn't care. But no alarm means we can take our time."

"Can you maybe be a little more cautious next time?" I asked

"Nope." She swung the door open and we walked inside. As soon as I felt safely hidden in the racks, I flicked on the light from my helmet. And froze.

There was so much choice. I just stood there, staring dumbly at row on row of potato chips, cookies, hot dogs, *real* chocolate bars. I had been on Perses so long I had forgotten what variety looked like. My mouth watered and my stomach grumbled.

Elena mumbled something.

"What?" I said.

Her cheeks were already crammed with some kind of smoked beef jerky. She took a giant gulp, then in a slightly more coherent way mumbled, "I said, 'Stop daydreaming. Let's get moving.'"

Fatima jumped behind the counter and threw large shopping bags at us. Even the rough cloth felt exotic.

I jammed my arm onto a shelf of cookies and swept the entire row into a bag. Then I slid it toward the door.

"We'll need protein and water too," I said, tossing more junk food into another bag. "But we might as well enjoy this trip."

"As much as we can," Fatima said.

In just minutes, we'd filled four giant bags each. Not just with food but also with clean shirts, jeans, and sweatpants. The rain had begun to come down even harder as we made our way back to the digger. The weight of the booty was tugging at my shoulders as I scurried through the water.

"No wonder there's no one around," I said, walking up next to Elena. "This is like a hurricane."

"I hope Mandeep isn't drowning down in the sewer," Elena said, not joking. We quickened our pace.

We were almost at the grate when a bolt of lightning struck a utility pole just a few feet from us. The light left me momentarily blinded. The thunder made my ears ring. I smashed right into Elena and we toppled over. My eyes adjusted. Cans of food rolled away down the street. I could taste blood on my lips. Fatima and Elena were staring, wide-eyed, as they watched the cans roll into the distance.

"Sorry," I said.

"It's not that," Elena said, pointing off toward the east. "We've got company."

Headlights cut through the rain, approaching quickly. "Stay low," I yelled. I began crawling toward the grate as quickly as I could, hauling the bags behind me.

The ground shook and rumbled as the trucks or tanks grew closer. There was no way to tell if it was Thatcher's troops, the police, or just a truckload of locals.

We reached the grate, the water pouring down like a waterfall. I stared down the hole. The tunnel was filling up fast, the water rushing through it like a rapid.

And Mandeep was gone.

Elena joined me. "Damn," she said.

"Can't we jump in?" Fatima asked.

"We'll drown."

The headlights of a large truck were now on us. The truck began to slow. No doubt we'd been spotted. "GO!" I yelled.

We leaped up, leaving the bags of precious food, and began to run. *"Pare!* Stop!" yelled a voice. We ran faster, the truck now swerving to follow, the lights fully on our backs, our shadows seeming to grow as they raced ahead of us. There were no gaps between the buildings, no parks or woods where we could dash and hide.

I waited for the explosion of a blaster in my back.

Lightning struck a building to our left, sending sparks flying through the air. I turned. The truck was just a few feet away. A woman's face in the windshield. Her hands gripping the wheel, her eyes locked on to us.

I had seen her before. When we'd landed. She was one of the grinders who'd helped us escape. She'd waved at us as we'd sped by in the digger. She was waving at me again now, trying to get my attention.

I stopped. "Wait!" I yelled to the others. "She's not an enemy. She's a . . ."

There was a loud squeal and then the sound of ripping metal. The road buckled and cracked at my feet, throwing me to the ground. I rolled to my side, sure the truck was about to crush me. I looked back. The truck was lying on its side, sliding along the road toward one of the nearby buildings.

It seemed to move in slow motion, relentlessly, until with a loud crash it went right through the front window of a store. Then, silence. It lay there like a dead animal, its wheels spinning.

Shattered glass was strewn across the street. Where the truck had been was a large hole . . . and our digger.

Mandeep pulled up next to us, the digger's nose cone sending off clouds of steam.

She opened the cockpit lid. "I hit the rear of the truck," she said. "Knocked it sideways." She seemed shaken— happy but also shocked at what she'd just done.

Fatima made her way over to the wreckage first. The woman crawled through the window of the twisted cab, her hands and arms cut and burned. Blood flowed from a gash on her forehead. "She needs help," she said. Then she gave a loud gasp.

The woman's bare arm clearly displayed her double-M tattoo.

"I am here to help you," the woman said. Then she went limp.

Chapter Twenty-Four

Help

We searched every building, frantically looting medical supplies, clothes, anything we could use. We were loud and fast. There was no longer any need to be careful.

The wreckage of a transport truck, the unmistakable hole of a digger blasting through rock? Dead giveaways. Someone must have heard or seen the explosion and called whatever authorities were nearby. And that meant, ultimately, Thatcher.

Mandeep was doing her best to treat the woman. She'd yanked the seat cushion out of the truck and set it on the sidewalk.

So far the woman was too weak to say anything

more, even her name. The rest of us began packing the digger with our stolen supplies. I kept stealing nervous looks at the sky and the intersecting roads.

The rain had now given way to thick fog, the air changing from warm and wet to clammy and heavy.

"You recognized her?" Fatima asked as she handed me a blaster we'd grabbed from the wreckage of the truck.

"Too late," I said. "But yes. She was one of the grinder soldiers who helped us escape."

Fatima's eyes opened wide. "The one who waved at us."

I nodded. "But I don't think she was actually waving."

"Explain," Elena said, jamming a small handheld blaster into the pocket of her new pants.

The wave had bugged me then, and it had nagged at me since. It was too strange a gesture. A friendly wave in the middle of such violence?

No. She'd been doing something else. I walked over to the digger and felt along the bottom until my fingers came across a tiny metal disc, no bigger than a small coin, stuck to the hull just over the rear tracks. I grabbed a screwdriver from the tool kit and struggled to pull it off the metal. It finally came loose with an audible click and fell into my hand.

"Magnetic tracking device," I said.

Fatima came over and took it, holding it up to the light. "She threw it onto our digger when we were escaping. Maybe Thatcher's troops did the same thing?" Her eyes darted around, as if expecting armed troops to emerge from the fog.

Elena shook her head. "They would have tracked us by now."

Fatima calmed down. But she seemed more agitated than I'd ever seen her. Jumpy and nervous. I was so used to seeing her so calm and in control.

"What's wrong?" I asked.

Her eyes looked down, then back at me. "I don't know. It's just strange meeting a grinder rebel. I have so many questions."

A bird began singing somewhere in the distance. "The sun is almost up," I said. "We have to move."

"Chris! She's awake!" Mandeep called. We hurried over. The woman looked horrible. Her leg sat at an odd angle. Her left eye was swollen shut.

"We're so sorry," I said.

"I . . ." She tried to speak but her voice was so low I could barely hear it.

I knelt down and leaned in close, my ear almost touching her mouth.

"People knew you were coming back," she said. "Good people."

She paused to lick her lips, groaning as if even that hurt. "A safe place . . ." Her voice trailed off. Mandeep gave her a sip of water. More birds were singing. I began to worry about time.

"Place?" I asked.

She lifted her head. "The Opening is near."

"The opening? I'm sorry. I don't understand."

"Use nothing as your guide."

Now I was totally lost. "Please help . . . explain."

The woman kept her head up, shaking with the effort, and looked at Fatima, who knelt down beside me. "Opening," she repeated. "Underground. You know?"

"Yes," Fatima said. She took the woman's hands in hers. "Opening. Underground. Tell me."

They began a conversation, but not one I could follow. Some words were in different languages. Some were terms that sounded familiar—nothing, guide, moon—but which made no sense the way they used them. The woman lost a little more of her energy as she pushed each word out. Then she leaned back in Mandeep's arms, spent.

Fatima stood up and nodded firmly at the woman. "The Opening is under the sun and moon, at night. And we use nothing as our guide."

The woman nodded, then coughed. "That is all I know."

"I understand, and thank you." Fatima bent down and kissed the woman's forehead. Then she stood and walked back to the digger without another word. She closed the trunk and opened the cockpit lid.

"Fatima?" I called. But she didn't turn around.

I looked back at the woman. She was looking at her watch.

"I'm sorry we attacked you," I said. "We thought you were with . . ."

"Thatcher," she said, nodding slightly. "Stay suspicious." She reached over and pushed a button on the watch, then relaxed back onto the cushion. "Stay suspicious."

"We'll take you to your friends," I said. "They can help you get better."

The woman shook her head. "No. Go," she said. "Find the Opening." A red light on her watch began to pulse. It wasn't a watch at all. It was a detonator. The truck was booby-trapped!

I reached down and placed my arms under her shoulders, lifting her back.

I'd left so many people behind. I'd left Pavel, a traitor, and still I felt sick about it. I wasn't going to leave her. A friend.

"No!" she said. I ignored her. Fatima was already inside the digger. Didn't she care?

The detonator continued to flash. Mandeep tried to help.

"No," the woman said again. "Hurry!"

Elena grabbed the woman's legs and we struggled to lift her. Incredibly, she began kicking, fighting us, each attempt to break our grip causing a spasm of pain through her body.

"No," the woman said through gritted teeth. "You. Must. Go." She sounded just like Nazeem before Thatcher had arrived to execute him. Ordering us, imploring us to leave.

There was a low rumble from deep in the fog. Something big was coming, fast.

"Go," the woman said. Then there was a snap from her mouth, like someone breaking a stick in half.

"NO!" Mandeep said, looking up at me desperately. "I think she bit a poison pill."

There was a rattle in the woman's throat and flecks of white foam broke through her lips. "Go," she said. Then her eyes rolled back in her head. Her watch began to blink faster. She was gone.

We lay her body back on the cushion.

A red flash cut through the air over our heads, blasting the top of a nearby tree, which burst into flames. I looked up just as a huge truck turned the corner at the end of the road. A dozen or more soldiers hung from the sides, blasters drawn.

We turned and ran just as the grinder's truck exploded, sending a plume of flame and smoke into the air. The force knocked us flat. Shards of red-hot metal rained down around us. Had the explosion taken out the troops as well? I dared to hope.

But with a roar, the truck crashed through the fiery wreck.

We got up and ran for the digger.

In just moments we'd be run over, or shot.

Elena stepped in the middle of the road in front of us. She spread her legs and raised her blaster. She was as far from me as my mother had been when the Landers had killed her.

"Elena!" I called. "Move!"

She didn't move. Two blasts hit the road on either side of her, sending bits of molten asphalt flying. She didn't flinch. The truck was now about a hundred yards away. More soldiers raised their blasters.

"Elena! Run!" I yelled, reaching her. I tried to grab her arm as I passed, but she swatted my hand away, keeping the blaster raised with the other.

"I'll be right there."

I just stared at her as Mandeep gripped my shoulder and pulled me toward the nearby digger. We climbed inside as another blast boomed into the ground by Elena's leg. She flinched only slightly, the shrapnel ripping a hole in her pants.

The truck was almost on top of her.

Elena squeezed the trigger. The blast hit the truck square in the front and the cab erupted in flames. The truck swerved violently, flipped, and smashed into the curb. Soldiers were thrown around like rag dolls.

Elena turned and ran over to us and leaped inside the cockpit. A few soldiers were finding their bearings, scanning the scene for us.

I closed the cockpit, hacking; my lungs burned.

Fatima didn't hesitate. In a flash she'd fired up the machine and we cut back down into the ground.

We'd escaped, narrowly.

"That was pretty epic," Mandeep said, patting Elena on the back.

"And pretty stupid," I said.

Elena smoothed her pant leg. "I said it on Perses and it's the same here on Earth. I'm done hiding. When they fight, we fight."

Fatima headed straight down, then executed a complete turn so we faced the direction we'd just come from. She blasted the tunnel closed. Then she turned off the digger.

"The guidance system is calibrated to Earth now," she said. "The woman told me there was a way to switch it."

The map glowed on the screen, no longer useless. It showed completely different lines and the contours of lakes, roads, and rivers.

"That's excellent!" I said.

Fatima stared straight ahead, stone-faced. "Elena. Can you take over? I need to do some thinking."

"Sure," Elena said. She slid over Fatima's lap and behind the steering column, then pulled the digger away. We sped toward what our compass said was the east.

I was still confused about the conversation between the grinder and Fatima, but I was more worried about Fatima's demeanor.

"You okay?" I asked.

She didn't answer.

"You hurt?" Mandeep asked.

Fatima made a sucking sound with her lips. "No." She paused a long time, her lips set in a straight line, her arms crossed. She stared straight out the window. "That woman was the first grinder we've met face-to-face, and she is dead because of us. We killed her."

Mandeep looked down, silent.

"It's not our fault," I said. "We thought she was trying to kill us. We had no way to know she wasn't with Thatcher."

"*She,*" Fatima said. "We never even found out her name." Then she closed her eyes and leaned back in the seat.

Elena continued to dig, and we all sat in silence as we ran, safely surrounded by rock.

Chapter Twenty-Five

Open

I was startled awake by Fatima talking loudly in her sleep.

"Night! Night! Night!" Her blankets rustled in the darkness.

I sat up, hurriedly turning on my headlamp, my heart pounding like a hammer.

"Fatima, wake up." I reached over to nudge her.

Fatima was lying on a blanket just a foot away, her eyes still closed, her arms and legs tensed. "NIGHT!" she yelled. The sound echoed off the tunnel walls.

Mandeep woke with a shriek and rolled behind the digger.

Elena grabbed her blaster and leaped up, ready to fire.

"It's okay," I said. "Fatima's just having a nightmare." I leaned over and shook Fatima harder. She woke up with a gasp.

Mandeep looked around from behind the nose cone.

Elena relaxed a little but continued to wave the blaster around the room.

"Sorry, everyone," Fatima said, rubbing her eyes.

"Nightmare?" Mandeep asked.

"Some memories. I didn't even know I had them," Fatima said. "About my first few weeks as a grinder. It was horrible." She rubbed her eyes. "You guys go back to sleep."

Elena put down her blaster. "Don't think that's going to happen."

"Might help to tell us about it," I said.

"It must have been triggered by some stuff the woman and I talked about."

"The opening?" I asked.

"Yeah. 'The Underground and the Opening.' It's a kind of legend, or fairytale. Or at least I thought it was. A story grinders tell each other to give ourselves some hope, about this whole series of secret tunnels and safe houses. A way for grinders to escape."

"But it's *not* just a story?"

Fatima shook her head. "She told me where the

Opening was. She knew she was dying. She had been coming to tell us where to go next."

"So where is that?" Mandeep asked.

"That's the weird part," Fatima said. "It was like she didn't know. Like she'd never seen it herself. She said she'd been given a message about the sun and the moon at night. 'Use nothing as your guide.' She repeated it like she had it memorized. Like she didn't actually know what it meant."

Elena sighed. "Sounds like we're in the same boat."

Fatima ran a hand through her hair, frustrated. "It's clearly a code of some kind. I just don't know exactly what it means. We need the key to decipher it."

"Great," I said, instantly regretting the sarcasm in my voice. "I mean it *is* great. We just have to figure it out." But I was feeling irritable. This was the second cryptic puzzle we'd received. One, a set of useless numbers from the Oracle. Now this bizarre message about sun and moon and . . . Something flashed in my memory.

"Wait," I said. "She said underground, right?"

Fatima nodded.

I closed my eyes and rubbed my forehead. Something the Oracle had said in her last transmission came back to me. After giving me the sequence of numbers, she'd said she had to go to the underground. I'd just assumed she meant she needed to hide again. What if she meant THE Underground?

Ever since the Blackout, we'd been having to figure out the big picture with just a piece of the puzzle at a time. But every step had been on purpose. My father had left me a code I needed to crack so that no one else could know where the beacon was hidden.

The Oracle had waited until we'd figured out the code on the beacon, in my mother's handwriting, before sending us sensitive information.

"It's another double-blind," I said at last.

"A double-what?" Fatima looked at me, confused.

"Two people have one half of a secret message. Each half is useless without the other. Neither person knows the other half. My mom and dad used to leave notes for each other like that. It was a game."

Now everyone was staring at me silently, waiting.

"The Oracle gave me *half* of the message. The numbers that I thought were the entry code. That was the only half she knew. But then she left me a clue that it had something to do with the Underground."

"That seems like a huge risk," Elena said, raising an eyebrow. "We know Thatcher's people were listening."

"Maybe. But even if his troops knew it was about the

Underground, the code is still useless without the other half of the message."

"Which is the stuff about the sun and moon?" Mandeep asked.

"Yes. The grinder woman only knew that half of the combination. So in case *she* got caught and they got the message from her, it would be useless. They'd still have no idea what it was."

Elena looked at each of us in turn, then back at me. "So the Oracle was working with the grinders."

"As we suspected. That's how they knew where and when we would land. The woman was probably supposed to give us the other half of the code then."

Fatima frowned. "But we escaped before she could, so she came after us."

"And now we are the only four people on Earth who have both sides of the message," Elena said.

"Yes."

She stared straight at me. "So?"

I gave a loud sigh. "And I don't know how they go together yet. What did the woman say, exactly?"

Fatima closed her eyes and concentrated. "We switched languages a couple of times and she threw in some grinder lingo. But basically it was that the

Opening was under the stars. And it would take us between the sun and the moon at night. That's the part that confused me because the sun isn't out at night. But she kept repeating it."

Mandeep and Elena asked Fatima some more questions, but I wasn't listening anymore.

My mind had started working. I liked numbers and codes, and now that I could at least try to fit them together, I was making progress. The numbers the Oracle had given me and the message the woman had left us were connected.

But how? And what were they saying?

45. 91. 39. 10. 75. 22.

In grinder codes there was always a hidden sequence. Some of the numbers were extra, useless, misdirections. But if you figured out the key, you could determine which numbers were right, and which would send you hundreds of miles away from your target.

The clue had to be in the grinder's last words.

The woman had told Fatima and me to use "nothing as your guide," and that the opening was under "the sun and the moon at night." Fatima had said that was impossible. Except, I realized with a jolt, now, in summer, when the Earth was tilted on its axis. Then the sun and the moon are out at the same time, at night, in the northern hemisphere.

North! That was the key.

I ran the numbers through my head.

45. 91. 39. 10. 75. 22.

"Use nothing as your guide." That was the other part of the formula the woman had told Fatima to remember.

Nothing.

Nothing.

What was "nothing" when it came to directions?

In a minute, I had it, or hoped I did.

Nothing meant zero.

That could mean the equator, zero latitude. It could also mean the prime meridian, zero longitude. If I was right about north, it could only be zero longitude. The equator never saw the sun at night.

The sequence would reveal the latitude. But which numbers worked? I knew right away I could throw out 91 degrees latitude, because it didn't exist. The poles were 90 degrees from the equator, and that was as far as you could go.

"I'm going to use the mapping on the computer for a second," I said.

"Got something?" Elena smiled.

"Maybe," I said, climbing into the cockpit.

I plugged the remaining numbers in one by one and looked up the line that connected them, the prime meridian.

39, 10, 75, and 22 all sat in the middle of huge bodies of water. *Red herrings,* I thought with a chuckle. *Appropriate for getting lost in the ocean.*

But 45 sat right in the middle of beautiful, secure, and easily-dug-into earth.

I stuck my head over the side of the cockpit.

"The Opening is close," I said.

"Seriously?" Elena looked skeptical. "You're a smarty pants, Chris, but that seems fast even for you."

"The Oracle's numbers." I pointed to the dashboard. "And if my calculations are right, we're almost there."

Chapter Twenty-Six
Stars

Elena had said we needed to run silent and run deep, and she was right. We went deep. But that meant we were often sluggish, tired, and hot—doing our best to ration the oxygen masks when the internal air supply in the digger got low. Whoever drove got one the whole time. The rest of us sort of lolled on the seat like zombies.

I thought back to that book Elena had read on the flight home, about living in extreme conditions. This was like living at high altitude. Low oxygen was not natural or healthy, and we were fighting an ongoing battle between feeling perpetually tired and perpetually nauseous.

"What does the map say?" I asked Elena, who was driving. My head rested on her shoulder, which felt nice.

"We're almost underneath the coordinates now," she said.

I forced my eyes to focus on the dashboard monitor. We stopped on 45 degrees latitude, still surrounded by solid rock.

"You sure we're close?" Mandeep asked.

"It's got to be up or down from here," I said.

Elena turned the nose up. "I highly doubt it's lower than we are, so let's see what's closer to the surface."

We began climbing.

Suddenly, we flew into open space. The digger rose up, then tipped and fell to the ground with a thud. The disrupter shut off and the digger bounced to a stop.

The room was immediately flooded with blinding white light. My eyes screamed in pain.

"Move!" Fatima yelled.

"I'm trying!" Elena said. "Something's got us!"

The drill spun and squealed but the digger stayed still.

My eyes adjusted. We were in an enormous cave. Floodlights mounted on the ceiling were shining down on us from all sides. Metal cables with some kind of magnetic caps or suction were attached to the hull of the digger.

Elena reached down to ignite the disrupter, using

the override that would blow up the entire room, including us.

"No," I said. "Not yet."

"It's a trap!" Elena said, her finger hovering near the switch.

"What do we do?" Mandeep asked, desperately grasping for one of the small blasters we kept hidden under the seat.

A man with a large blaster approached the front of the digger, his face covered with a mask.

His voice came crackling over the digger's emergency frequency, a trick Thatcher had used on Perses.

"Open the cockpit and put your hands up."

Fatima clenched her fists and spat. "I'll show him what 'hands up' means to a grinder."

The man stopped about five feet from the front of the digger. He lowered his weapon, which fell to his side, held by a shoulder strap.

Elena motioned with her eyes for me to grab the blaster from her pocket. I tried to reach over as carefully as possible.

The man gave a deep sigh, clearly audible over the speaker. He shook his head and then rolled up the sleeve on his right arm, revealing the unmistakable double-M brand of the Melming Mining Corporation.

Fatima relaxed and unclenched her fists.

Mandeep let out a long breath.

Elena leaned back, her hand pushing mine before I could grab the gun.

His voice came across the radio. "My name is Beca. Welcome to the Opening."

"This food is amazing," Fatima said as she used her fingers to scoop up some kind of rich green sauce with torn pieces of thin bread.

"Injera," Beca said, lifting a scoop of meat into his mouth. He was so good at it he barely got any of the sauce on his fingers, whereas I had goops dripping down my chin. And I didn't care one bit.

"It's . . . wow," Mandeep said. "Not quite as spicy as I usually like my grub, but it beats the canned sawdust we've been living on."

Beca nodded in thanks.

"So what is this place?" I asked. "The woman, the grinder who died . . . she sent us here."

He paused, just a split second. "So she is dead?"

"Yes. We assumed she was with Thatcher, so we fought back. She got hurt. Badly. Then she bit down on some kind of poison pill or something rather than be captured by Thatcher's troops."

"She was my sister." He'd said it so quietly I'd almost missed it. I tensed. Beca still had his blaster swung across his shoulder and I'd just told him we'd attacked his sister.

Elena, sitting next to me, glanced down at the blaster in her pocket.

But Beca raised his head without any sign of anger, just sadness in his eyes and voice. "She told me she might not come back many times. This time she was right."

"We've all lost people," I said. "We're so sorry. It wasn't . . ." I stumbled to try to say something to make it better.

"We are at war." He looked straight at me. "She knew the risks. There was no other way to contact you. She could just as easily have become a victim of Thatcher's goons. And she succeeded. You are here."

Elena relaxed. I felt horrible, but at least I didn't feel in danger.

"Was she the Oracle?" I asked.

Beca looked confused. "The who?"

"Sorry. The Oracle is what we called the woman who was sending us messages. The one who had answered our distress call from Perses."

"Ah," Beca said. "No. But Eden, my sister, *was* one

of the leaders of our rebellion." He looked down. "An excellent leader. But she had not contacted you before you arrived here on Earth."

"Her name was Eden?" Fatima asked.

Beca nodded. Fatima sat back against the wall. "Poor Eden," she said.

"She was a grinder, like you," Beca said. "She had worked as a mason, after being freed. We were never fully accepted in the outside world, but we were not hated. Then Thatcher began his campaign and someone saw her brand . . ."

"And she was let go," Elena finished.

"We'd been sold together, as twins, into service, when we were just eight years old. But then Melming split us up. She worked for years in a mine in South Africa. I was sent to this place." He gestured to the ceiling and the many tunnels that branched off from the walls. "It was a mine, until it went dry."

"Now it's the Opening?"

Beca smiled. "For you, today, yes. But the Opening isn't just one place. It has to change, move. We grinders can always find it, working together. And who knows better than us how to move underground? There's no map, at least not a written one," Beca said. "But it's all in here, and here." He touched his head and heart.

"Melming Mining doesn't remember a fraction of the tunnels we helped build on Earth."

"So this is only the Opening once?" I asked.

"Yes. And it leads to many tunnels. Some old, some new. Some that you will dig yourselves. There is a network of safe places, even some people, who will help you escape. But we have to move them often."

"So we can't be tracked easily when we are in the Underground?"

"These tunnels are very deep. They had to be. We dug deeper and deeper as Earth ran out of resources. We once used the Underground to help other grinders escape the clutches of Melming Mining. Now we use it to hide from everyone up top. Thatcher has made us hated. Scapegoats. Now we have to hide to survive."

"Sounds familiar," Elena said.

"And to fight back," Beca said.

"Also sounds familiar," Fatima said.

We ate in silence for a while. A pebble dislodged somewhere in the distance, sending down a *plink* that echoed off the tunnel walls. I flinched, but Beca didn't seem concerned, so I relaxed.

"How many tunnels are there on Earth?" I asked.

"Many. This old planet is almost empty of resources now. Perses was supposed to be a new hope," he said, with a small, hollow laugh. "Instead it was an old story."

"We're sorry," I said. "All that ore, destroyed. We were just trying to stop the Landers."

Beca scoffed. "That's not why I laughed. You think the Landers were bringing that ore back to Earth to share? No. Melming himself might have, when he was in charge. But that was a long time ago. Thatcher and his cronies have been seizing more and more control . . . and they do not share."

"And people just let them?" Elena asked, furious.

"Not everyone," Beca said, looking at each of us in turn. "People such as your parents saw what was happening. They hoped for better but prepared for the worst."

"Did you know my father?" I could feel a lump rise in my throat.

"We knew of him. He worked in the mines when we were all just children. He saw both sides of the company. Both sides of this world, in a way. Some of us suspect he and the others were sent to Perses as a precaution. To isolate a threat to Thatcher's plans."

"And when they left for Perses, he and some of the others set up a warning system here on Earth?"

Beca nodded. "Your father. Elena's father. Finn's mother. Mandeep's mother. And others. They did not tell anyone at Melming."

"How do you know all our names already?" Mandeep asked. She was right. We hadn't actually introduced ourselves before rushing to eat.

Beca smiled a huge smile and laughed. "You are famous. 'The first colonists of Perses.' There was a lot of anger when news of the Blackout attacks reached us. When the news of your deaths reached Earth."

"Our deaths?"

Beca nodded again. "The world thinks you were all killed. It would be very inconvenient to have you suddenly appear, very much alive, here on Earth."

"Like ghosts," Elena said.

"Thatcher isn't about to broadcast the fact that we are here, is he?" Fatima said.

"No. That would lead to some very troublesome questions. He wants you dead, needs you to be dead, and he will track you down himself. But he can't risk anyone in the general public finding out."

"Why don't we just go public now?" Mandeep asked, standing up suddenly—like she was ready to charge to the surface that second.

Beca held up his hand. "Go slowly. It sounds easy, but let's say you surface in a village or city and avoid meeting soldiers and even land among people who are sympathetic. Then what? Tell them your story? Good.

Then you have a handful of people who know the truth. Then the soldiers will arrive. They'll kill you, kill all the witnesses. Blame the grinders for that as well."

"Beca's right," I said. "We're only going to get one shot. We need to make it count. We have to get it right."

We sat for a while, chewing our food, considering this.

Elena broke the silence. "You said people were angry when they heard we were killed. Who were they angry at?"

"The grinders, of course. That's who Thatcher blamed. The saddest thing was how easily everyone believed him. Many of us have been jailed, or worse, just for having the tattoo. So we have decided it is time to fight back. It's also why we need you so much."

"Witnesses," Fatima said. "The only people who can say what happened on Perses and be believed."

"We can help vindicate the grinders," Mandeep said

Beca stood up, wiping his hands on his pant legs. "Which is why we need to get you somewhere where the *world* can see you, and hear you."

"And we have a lot to say," I said.

"The Underground will help you get where you need to go."

"Why not just tell us where that is?" Fatima asked. "We could go straight there."

"I only know how to tell you where to go next," Beca said.

"And where is that?" Elena asked. "Exactly?"

"I didn't say I knew. I said I knew *how* to tell you." Beca held out an ancient phone. Its screen was cracked and chipped. He pushed a button and it sprang to life. There was a short burst of some kind of music, and then a series of numbers appeared.

"The Oracle you mentioned gave you the coordinates for here. I'm sending you *here*." He held up the phone. "I cannot look at the screen. Do you see the numbers? They will only appear once and only for a few seconds."

I looked at them, memorizing them.

48

2

"Do you know the numbers?"

"Yes."

He slipped the back of the phone off and the battery fell out. Then he took the butt of his blaster and smashed the phone into tiny pieces.

"So who sent you those numbers?" Elena asked. She was clearly impatient to finish this. "Who knows the whole plan? Someone has to."

"I do not know where a final stop is, or even if there is one."

"Great," Elena said. She got up and paced the room, her frustration barely contained.

Beca followed her with his eyes. "The Underground is designed to keep you hidden and safe. But it is not like a map."

Elena continued pacing. "But who sent the numbers to this phone?"

"Whoever is at the next safe place. Perhaps it is this Oracle. They determine the location. Then it is sent from a phone there to this one. Both phones have now been destroyed."

"Why didn't you look?" I asked.

"I stay here, guarding this location until you go. If I am discovered I will die, like my sister, doing my job. But keeping me in the dark means there is no risk that I can reveal your location if I am caught."

I walked up to Beca and held out my hand. He took it, then captured me in a bear hug.

"You should get some sleep," he said.

"Yes. But before I do . . . are there more of those old phones around?"

"We have hundreds hidden in the tunnels. The salvaged garbage of a bygone time, but useful to us. Why?"

A hint of a smile played on my lips. "I have an idea."

Chapter Twenty-Seven
Halfway

We got a full night's sleep for the first time in recent memory. Elena wanted to stay up to keep an eye on Beca "just to be careful," but she soon fell asleep. When we woke, Beca was gone. In his place there were fresh oxygen tanks, food, and clothes—not overalls, but fresh T-shirts and pants.

We changed, packed quickly and quietly, and sped away into the solid rock wall.

"So any idea where we are actually heading?" Elena asked. She was still agitated. Still itching, I could tell, for a fight. Firing at the truck had whet her appetite for battle.

"I don't know what it is, but I know that Beca said it was the next stop on the Underground."

"How many stops until the last stop?" Mandeep asked. "If there actually is one."

I shrugged. "I don't think we'll know until we're there."

"I half hope we meet Thatcher before then," Elena said, turning slightly east.

"Why are you so impatient?" Mandeep asked.

"Because Thatcher's winning a battle and we aren't even fighting," Elena growled. "The longer we run, the more time Thatcher has to prepare, try to guess where we're heading. Try to stop us. I want to end this. I want to end *him*."

Mandeep went back to staring out the window.

Fatima had been silent for most of the trip, lost in thought. It must have been so hard, meeting grinders here on Earth. And then hearing Beca describe how quickly people had turned against them . . . I could share her anger but only sense a part of how horrible she must feel.

I touched her shoulder, but she pulled away and looked at me. "What was the point of all the cell phone stuff you and Beca were doing?"

I pointed at the screen on the dashboard. "We made a copy of the video on his phone. And then he'll make lots more."

"Why?"

"Backup. Every grinder with a phone will see it and have it."

She looked back out the window. "But the grinders will have no power to use it. And no people who will listen to them."

"I'm sorry," I said. "This isn—"

But she raised a hand to stop me, then closed her eyes and leaned back. In just a few seconds, she was asleep.

"I guess when you grow up underground, you can pretty much sleep anywhere, anytime," Elena whispered.

"Yeah," I said.

"The rocking of the digger is actually kind of soothing," Mandeep said. And, despite a full night's sleep, she was soon dozing as well.

"You don't think the oxygen tanks Beca gave us are faulty, do you?" I asked, stifling a yawn.

"I'm wide awake," Elena said, whispering just loud enough to be heard over the digger. "I think it's just a reaction to the stress."

"Maybe. Of course, you like stress."

She looked at me and smirked. "I've just gotten used to it."

"No kidding."

We drove on in silence for a while, the only sound the heavy breathing of our two sleeping passengers. I had almost nodded off too when Elena poked me in the side.

"Don't fall asleep on me, Fearless. This is our first chance to talk alone in a while," she said.

"Okay," I said, feeling a bit nervous. What did she want to talk about "alone"?

"Why do you think Thatcher hasn't been coming after us with diggers?"

Ah. Strategy. Of course.

But Elena knew me well enough to know I'd been thinking about it too. "Beca is right. Thatcher doesn't want to attract any attention to us. And as we've discovered, diggers are not the most reliable modes of transportation down here."

She considered this and, not surprisingly, disagreed. "No. Sorry. I think he wants us to keep going. He's hoping to capture us eventually, but he also wants to find whoever is helping us along the way."

"You think he was following us to the Opening?"

"I think there's a reason Beca wasn't there when we woke up. That place was compromised. I pretended to be asleep, but I saw him stringing up blaster caps all over the ceiling. The second we were gone, that place was done."

"How would he trigger that?"

Elena reached into her pocket and pulled out another tracking disc. "This was conveniently tucked into your pocket. I grabbed it when you were sleeping."

I thought of the hug Beca had given me the night before. "Dammit," I said. "You don't think he's a spy, do you?"

"No," Elena said. "I think he is being cautious. Once we passed through the wall, it set off the timer for the explosives."

"And he's tracking us now. To make sure we are on the move."

"Maybe. But I bet it's only short-range. Still . . ." Elena slowed the digger, then opened the cockpit just a touch. Bits of disintegrated rubble cascaded into my face, and she threw the homing device out the window. "Better safe than sorry. Don't want that signal picked up by anybody else."

She closed the lid.

"So you think both sides want us alive."

"Now, yes. But Thatcher was ready to have us killed the second we landed. The grinders saved us, and spooked him. That was organized. Well thought-out."

"Maybe they killed him in the attack?"

"I hoped that too. Until some of his goons showed up and came after us in that village."

"But they were really after Eden. That's why they were shooting at her truck."

"And not at us." Elena gave me a wink.

"Thatcher doesn't see us as an immediate threat."

"As long as we stay underground, only he and his cronies know that we're here on Earth."

"And the grinders who are helping us. So if he can use us to flush them out, then kill us after, he's taken care of his two biggest problems."

Elena nodded. "I think this grinder rebellion is doing more damage to him than he let on."

"This is good news, right?" I said. "It means, from a military perspective, as you like to call it, he's vulnerable."

"That's why he decided to go to Perses himself. To come back a hero, having crushed the rebellion." She grinned. "How'd that work out for him?"

"So the video of him killing Nazeem, and just us being here to talk about it, is lethal for him. But only if we can somehow tell millions of people."

"Instead of just a handful. Beca was right about that."

"We need more than just a few witnesses."

"Yeah."

"So we have to make sure we get those images to as many people as possible."

"Beca might do that with the phones."

"I doubt it," I said. "Those are old devices. They talk to each other, but unless you hand it to someone, it's only on the phones. I had Beca film the video so there'd at least be something left in case we get . . ." I left the rest unsaid.

"We need to find the Oracle."

"Why?"

"The Oracle reached us electronically—using long-range radio, short-range radio, interstellar radio—successfully. She has access to some kind of mobile receiver. And she knows how to use it, like a pro," Elena said. "She can get the word out."

"We know she's connected to the rebellion some-how," I said. "She's the one who sent us to the Opening."

"But Beca said he didn't know who she was, or where."

"Well, we're almost at the next stop. Maybe we can ask whoever is there."

Mandeep said something in her sleep and rolled over, nudging Fatima, who woke up.

"Are we there yet?" she asked, her voice groggy.

"Almost," Elena said. She began to slow the digger as the console showed us approaching the coordinates I'd seen on Beca's phone.

"Good idea," I said. "Last time was a bit of a jolt. I think we'll take things a little more slowly this time."

Fatima shook Mandeep awake. "Get ready," she said. We strapped on our helmets.

We were basically living entirely on trust at this point. Trust that the system Beca had shown us worked. Trust that Beca was who he said he was and that we would be safe at our next stop.

The map synced with the coordinates I'd plotted in, the numbers from Beca's phone, and the nose cone of the digger broke through into a dark tunnel. Elena stopped and flicked on the lights and the front camera. Particles of dust passed through the light beams, but everything else was indistinct.

"I don't see anything," she said.

"Or anyone."

She drove a few feet further and then stopped. The light had bounced off something on the far wall of the room.

"Zoom in," I said.

It was a small box, possibly another old phone. As we stared at it, a red light began to turn on and off, on and off. The screen came to life.

"Chris, that's a countdown," Elena said. "We gotta go!" She began to back the digger out of the hall.

"No," I said. "I need to see that phone."

"Are you crazy? It's going to blow up everything!"

"I need to see what's on the screen or we'll never find out where to go next."

Elena looked at me like I was insane, but I stared back. "Hurry!" I said.

"Argh." She fired up the front of the digger and drove across the room. Immediately, lights flooded the space, and Elena, blinded, didn't stop in time to avoid smashing into the far wall.

My forehead hit the dashboard with a thud and a loud crack, and everything began to swim. But even in the fog, I knew time was running out. I felt for the switch on the dashboard and opened the lid.

The phone wasn't just blinking; it was beeping.

Elena was moaning next to me. The digger engine had shut off.

I crawled over Elena and out of the digger, letting the beeping guide me to the phone.

I fumbled for it, and it slipped through my fingers and onto the floor.

I cursed.

But it continued to beep. My eyes were barely open, the light so bright it hurt to look. Finally, I was able to grab it and lift it to my face.

The numbers floated in a haze. I forced my eyes open, willing them to adjust.

The beeping began to speed up.

"Chris! Get back here!" It was Elena's voice.

I got up, stumbling on the uneven floor as I tried to shuffle back to the digger.

"Hurry!" Mandeep this time, her voice panicked.

Finally, the screen came into focus and I saw numbers. Just like the code on the phone Beca had shown me back at the Opening.

53.383

10.810

I repeated them to myself, then threw the phone, now beeping fast, as far away from me as I could.

I flew back to the digger and Fatima grabbed my arms. She pulled me inside just as the first explosion shook the far end of the room. A large chunk of the ceiling fell, crashing to the ground.

Elena fired up the digger and we escaped into the wall. There were more loud booms, shaking us even as we drove away.

I looked back. A giant fireball was racing toward us. Digger hull or no digger hull, we were about to be burned to a crisp.

"Turn right," I said.

Elena swerved so quickly we all banged our heads together.

The fire continued to follow us.

We turned and turned, the fire now licking at the trunk. But the farther and farther we got, the more the flames weakened.

We finally stopped. Elena was white as a ghost, her hands gripping the steering wheel so tightly the blood had drained from her knuckles.

"So I guess there's a time limit in getting from one safe space to the next."

"You think?" Fatima said.

"Might have been nice of Beca to warn us."

"We better get moving to the next one," I said.

"Oh no," Elena said.

"What?"

She pointed at the dashboard.

The screen was cracked where my helmet had hit it.

There was no way to tell where we were, or where we were going.

Chapter Twenty-Eight
Top

There was only one way to figure out where we were, and that was to hit the surface again. If I could see the sky, I could at least estimate where we needed to go. But would that leave time before the next locator blew up?

It was now daytime.

Surfacing in broad daylight was a perfect way to be seen, reported, captured, or killed. The people of Earth might have been angry that we were "killed" on Perses, but these were also the same people who were helping Thatcher hunt down and persecute grinders. The thought struck me . . . would I ever trust a stranger again?

"So where are we now? Approximately?" Elena asked, slowing but continuing to climb.

"The last coordinates would have put us in France." I thought back to the new numbers. "And we're supposed to head further east, toward Germany."

"But there's no way to tell which direction we're heading?" Fatima asked.

"We took so many turns to get away from that fireball, I'm not even sure we're heading *up*," Elena said.

"Lost again. Great." Mandeep punched the seat next to her.

"We're clearly heading up. Gravity and my inner ear tell me that much," I said as calmly as I could. "And we still seem to be cutting through rock, so that's good too. All we need to do is get up top and . . ."

"And what? Steal a compass?" Mandeep sounded angry, impatient.

I got it. "Look. I know this sucks. But we just have to keep moving."

Mandeep held out her hands in frustration. "Toward what? If Fatima and Elena are right, we're just leading everyone to the grinder cells. Or maybe Thatcher gets tired of that and decides he might as well whack us and end this whole 'problem.'"

Fatima jumped in. "Chris is right. There's no choice.

Even if they kill us, we can at least make sure that someone up top sees the video." She leaned forward and switched on the radio. "Or at least hears what Thatcher can do."

"Can't they track us using the radio?" Mandeep asked.

"Yes," I said. "If we say anything."

Fatima nodded. "Which we only do if we are attacked."

"An SOS?"

"No. A running play-by-play of whatever Thatcher's troops try to do to us. If they are shooting, we let them know they are shooting at kids."

Fatima was about to flick the switch off when the radio suddenly crackled to life. I practically jumped out of my seat.

"The latest from the drought in Asia. In other news . . ."

We'd stumbled into the middle of some kind of news report. It meant we were close enough to the surface to receive the signal. Elena slowed down.

"Still no word on the whereabouts of the terrorists who attacked a Melming Mining outpost in southern Europe."

Elena stopped driving and turned off the engine. We sat silently, staring at the console.

"Melming Mining asks everyone to be on the lookout for a Series Seven digger, stolen from the site. The terrorists are clearly identifiable by a double-M tattooed

on their arms. *Although reports suggest they may have tried to alter or erase this in some way. If spotted, do not approach. Call local authorities. They were last reported seen in southern France, near Arles.*"

"Well, that gives us some idea where we *were*," Fatima said.

"*General Kirk Thatcher, recently returned from a successful mission to Perses, had this to say.*"

"General?"

"Successful?"

Thatcher's raspy voice came over the speaker. I felt a cold shiver run down my spine.

"'*They are armed and very dangerous. They will stop at nothing to destroy our way of life. We will continue to scour the globe. These are members of the same grinder cell that attacked the mining colony on Perses. We killed the rebels there, and we will kill the remaining rebels here.*'"

Elena growled.

"'*I promise you this: We will find them. And we will hit them with so much firepower and fury, they will glow in the dark.*'"

Dozens of reporters began yelling questions and then the announcer returned.

"*Attacks have risen in frequency in recent months. The Global Government Council has given more emergency*

powers to General Thatcher and Melming Mining. A cur-
few has been imposed in southern Europe and northern
Africa. Anyone caught out after dark without a valid rea-
son will be detained. If you suspect anyone of being a
grinder, authorities have set up an anonymous report—"

Fatima switched off the radio and rubbed her forehead slowly. "Sorry. It's just making me sick."

Elena leaned across me and gave Fatima a gentle rub
on the shoulder.

"Thanks," Fatima said. "Scapegoating is just amazing,
isn't it?"

"Better than being attacked," Mandeep said.

"No, it's not," Fatima said, suddenly angry. "It poisons
everyone against a group, not just the people who think
they have to fight them. It makes the people in that group
less 'valuable,' even less than they were to start."

"Scapegoating is also a military strategy," Elena said.
"Attacks can rouse sympathy. But attacking an agreed-on
enemy, an enemy everyone believes is responsible for
all the bad in the world?"

"Whatever it takes is fine," Fatima said. "No more
rules. No need for mercy. That's why scapegoating is
worse than just attacking."

"Sorry," Mandeep almost whispered. "I guess I'm just
so frustrated."

"And scared," Fatima said.

Elena nodded. "We all are. Right, Chris?"

I stared at her. Elena rarely admitted any sign of weakness. But she was right. Admitting weakness to each other would make our bond stronger.

"Yes," I said. "A lot." Mandeep sat up a little straighter, her mouth set in a line.

Elena resumed digging, slowly, toward the surface. "We have to get moving. And we have to be careful."

"I wonder what Thatcher did with Pavel," Mandeep said.

The comment stung, even though she didn't mean it to. The image of Pavel's face begging us to take him still haunted me every night.

"Who cares," Elena said bitterly.

Fatima spoke up. "We should care. If he's a prisoner, he can talk. If he's dead, Thatcher can say 'grinders did it.' But he didn't say anything about Pavel, at least not in this report, so maybe he's alive."

"Or captured by the grinders," Mandeep suggested.

"I think Beca would have mentioned that," I said. "I just hope he's okay. No matter what, he was one of us."

"Until he chose not to be," Elena said quickly.

I had no answer for that.

Chapter Twenty-Nine
Plan B

For months an idea had been forming in my sub-conscious, a kind of conviction about where all this had to end. It had started as a small glimmer of hope on our flight to Earth, but something Beca said had made it come fully alive. And now, underground, lost and afraid, I knew it was time to share my thoughts with the others.

"I know where we need to go," I said.

"To see Hans Melming," Elena said, before I could.

I was too shocked to say anything.

"Your hero worship has never gone away, has it?" she said, smiling.

"It's not hero worship," I said. "Beca said that Melming

would have shared the shipments from Perses."

"He also said that was a long time ago," Elena said.

"Melming has to be like a zillion years old now," Fatima said.

"At least," Mandeep added.

"But he's the only person we KNOW we can trust."

Elena laughed. "Chris, you are being so naive. Melming is still around because Thatcher trusts him. Faking an old dude's death by natural causes wouldn't raise anyone's suspicions."

"No," I said. "Thatcher needs him. Melming gives Thatcher legitimacy, cover. He'll keep him around until he doesn't need that anymore. It's a sign that Thatcher doesn't have full control yet."

The others looked skeptical.

"I don't know," Mandeep said. "This seems like a long shot."

"Which is all we've had from the start."

Elena shut off the engine. She turned and stared at me. "Okay. Point taken. But what can Melming actually *do*?"

"Well, if he does still have credibility with world leaders and the 'people,' he could give that to us. He'd believe us, I'm sure. He could tell everyone what happened and no one could accuse him of lying." I felt like I was pleading a court case. "Trust me, any idealism

I had was killed on Perses. I'm not being naive. The Oracle told us months ago that Melming himself was always true to the original mission."

Elena tapped the steering column, thinking. Mandeep and Fatima furrowed their brows but didn't say anything.

"I'm being practical," I said. "We need to see Melming. There's no better option. Certainly not one that can offer us the global reach we need to make an actual difference."

"Fine," Elena said at last, sounding more resigned to the plan than supportive. "Any idea where he is?"

"Um . . . no."

"Great," she said.

"He used to live in Norway," I said feebly.

"A nice big country thousands of miles away." The sarcasm dripped from her voice. "With lots of water in between. We'll be there in time for dinner."

I sat back. She wasn't wrong. "We could drive underground the long way." Even I could hear how sulky I sounded.

Elena fired up the digger. "Let's solve our immediate problem. Where the heck are we now?"

She drove slowly again, moving forward and upward. "We're close enough to the surface to pick up radio signals. We must be close enough to a town with replacement parts."

"Like a new console screen," Mandeep said.

"Where are we going to find a digger up there?" Fatima asked.

"We're not," Elena said. "But there must be something that will work. We just need to find it."

About an hour later, after a few unplanned stops in sewage lines and an abandoned subway tunnel, we arrived under a busy street. A dim light shone through the storm drains and traffic hummed and buzzed above us.

Elena got out and scouted out the surroundings. "Just a normal road, maybe a small highway," she said. "The good news is there's some kind of restaurant across the way. Maybe we can steal some grub once the sun goes down."

My stomach rumbled. Beca's meal seemed ages ago. The tinned foods we had just reminded me of our rations on Perses. Therese and Darcy must have been able to plant and possibly harvest some food for themselves by now. I had to believe they had.

"Ironic, isn't it?" Fatima said as static began hissing over the radio.

"What?"

"Back on Earth. But back underground."

"Ironic and sad," I said.

Elena climbed into the cockpit. She sat down and began fiddling with the radio. "Let's try to change that situation right now." The radio cycled through more static, then stopped on a channel playing dance music. Elena shook her head and then swung the dial again.

"What are you looking for?" I asked.

"Anything that sounds official, military . . . whatever. We are sitting in an official Melming Mining vehicle. We must be able to access transmissions."

If Pavel had been here, we could have easily figured out which frequency to tune in to. Instead, we began scanning them one by one. I tried to force myself to ignore the ticking of each second. We had to be running late and the later we were, the less it mattered. Whatever underground safe place we were supposed to find next was inching closer to being nothing but exploded rubble.

Elena continued tuning. More static. More news reports. A weather report. Different languages. Different music. Then, finally, something clearly different. Numbers, chatter. A dispatcher and a truck driver.

"Dispatch. This is MM Six. En route to Base Echo with cargo. Moving ahead of schedule."

"Roger, MM Six. Rendezvous at fourteen hundred."

"Roger, dispatch. Over and out."

I wasn't sure what this gained us, exactly. "So we know there's a Melming truck somewhere in radio range. Now what?"

Elena looked at me and winked, then she turned on our microphone. "MM Six, this is MM Four. Do you copy?"

I reached over and flicked off the microphone. "Are you nuts?!?" I hissed.

"They can track us!" Mandeep said.

Elena didn't respond. She just sat there, her finger hovering over the microphone switch.

Finally after a few seconds of silence, an answer. *"MM Four. Back already?"*

Elena looked at me and smiled. "Luck happens, but you better be ready to make the opportunity count."

She flicked the microphone back on.

"Roger, MM Six. But having some tech difficulties." She switched the microphone on and off to mimic static interference. "Have stopped at Louwen Diner. Dispatch says you are close. Can you help? Over."

She closed her eyes, whispering, "C'mon, c'mon."

"Roger, MM Four. Close? Um, well . . . maybe." This was followed by an agonizing few seconds of static. I could almost see the driver deliberating over his

options. I hoped he wasn't also calling dispatch, or the real MM Four. Finally: *"Copy that. Can be there in ten. Over."*

I hadn't even noticed that we'd been holding our breath but all four of us exhaled at the same time.

Elena flicked on the mike. "Roger, MM Six. Much appreciated. Coffee on me. See you in ten. Over and out." She flicked off the radio, then let out a loud whoop.

I gave Elena a slug on the shoulder. "Nice work," I said.

"That was the easy part. Now we've got to get ready to grab that truck."

"Grab it?" Fatima asked.

"Well, the part we need."

"What's the plan?"

"Three of us need to head up top. One to keep an eye on our driver. One to keep watch. And one to grab the truck's GPS."

"You think he's going to leave it unlocked?" Fatima asked.

"No. I think we're going to break in, from underneath." She pointed at the radio, then turned to look at Mandeep.

"Mandeep, you keep an ear out. Any chatter at all between that truck and anyone else, and you get up top and get us the heck out of here."

"Wait, I'm driving?" Mandeep said. She looked nervous. "I don't know . . ."

But I could see what Elena had in mind. Mandeep had been in a funk ever since Eden had died. This was a way to turn that around. "Mandeep, we all saw what you did to that truck."

She flinched and looked away. "That was a mistake," she said.

I forged ahead. "No. That was an amazing maneuver. You did exactly what you had to do. And you can do this too."

Mandeep turned back to face me.

"It was amazing. Truly. Just dig up the same way, more slowly, and then into the cab of that truck."

Mandeep's eyes narrowed. Her lips pursed. Excellent.

"Okay," she said.

I smiled at her. "Awesome."

Elena opened the cockpit and jumped out. "We need to get going and we need to be superfast. Someone needs to keep that driver away from the truck."

Fatima cracked her knuckles. "I'm on it."

"Good," Elena said. She walked to the back of the digger. I heard the click of the trunk.

"I'll climb in through the hole," I said.

Elena came back into view, holding a blaster tight to

her chest. "And I'll make sure nobody gets in our way."

We drove underneath a nearby side street and climbed out of a rain gutter. "Two minutes until our pigeon arrives," Elena said, brushing dirt and dead leaves off her pants. Her blaster was concealed, as much as possible, under a large poncho we'd stolen from the store. That had only been a few days before, but it seemed so much longer.

We walked over to the main road as casually as we could manage. It was busier than I'd expected. Four lanes of traffic running in both directions. A mixture of almost every type of vehicle you could imagine, all traveling at top speed.

"I don't see a crossing," I said.

Elena was frowning, watching the traffic whiz by. "We'll have to make one," she said.

"Yeah. That's not going to raise any suspicions," Fatima joked.

Elena had begun counting out loud. "Ten. Nine. Eight."

"There he is!" Fatima yelled as a giant jet-blue truck began slowing to turn into the parking lot across the road.

"Get ready," Elena yelled.

"What?" I said, watching a huge trailer zoom by and almost run over my toes.

"Three. Two. One. NOW!" Elena started sprinting across the lanes.

Almost like we were carried in her wake, we followed. Cars, some with drivers, others autonomous, narrowly missed us as we ran, stopped, and started again trying to avoid getting hit.

"Why didn't we climb out over on *that* side?" Fatima yelled as we jumped away from one car and into the path of another, which swerved to avoid us.

"No cover," Elena said.

"THIS IS COVER!?!" Fatima said as we miraculously reached the meridian. Two more lanes to go. I could see the truck driver get out of his cab, looking around the parking lot for any sign of the broken-down MM Four. It wouldn't take him long to figure out he'd been duped. He walked toward the diner, but quickly.

He was about to discover that he was alone.

Meanwhile, Mandeep was going to start digging up inside the truck, and we'd be too far away to do anything.

"We're screwed," I said. The traffic seemed to build as I said this.

"Plan B," Elena said. She swung her poncho over her shoulder and took the blaster in her hands.

"What's plan B?" Fatima said. "We never talked about a plan B."

Elena took aim and fired a blast right into the back of the truck. The explosion sent the truck forward a good five feet, shattering the windows on both the cabin and the diner. Traffic stopped as the cars jammed on their brakes or reversed as quickly as they could. It was like Elena had parted the Red Sea.

"C'mon!" Elena yelled, sprinting across the road. We followed, no longer worrying about caution.

A blast came at us from inside the diner. The driver had found his wits and his weapon. Elena fired back, blowing out a chunk of the diner wall.

"Elena! There are innocent people in there!" I yelled.

"I'm only aiming for the guilty one," she yelled, firing higher, hitting the roof, and sending a shower of concrete and shattered cinder block raining down. The front door was now entirely blocked by rubble.

We reached the back of the truck, using it as cover. Smoke was billowing over our heads.

"Just so you know, plan B sucks!" I yelled over all the noise.

"Just get inside the cab," Elena yelled. She knelt down and stuck the blaster around the side of the truck, continuing to fire at the front of the building.

Sirens began to wail in the distance.

Fatima and I hurried around to the driver's side of the

cab. I used the foothold of the truck to pull myself up. Peering through the shattered window, I could see the front of the diner collapsing in larger and larger chunks as Elena continued firing. Scared customers ran out the back door, but the driver continued to fire blindly from behind the wall of debris.

I scrambled inside the cab.

There was no need for Mandeep to cut into the truck anymore, but as soon as I realized that, the floor began to vibrate. Mandeep was cutting up and into the soft bottom of the truck. I poked my head out the window.

"Fatima, get her attention somehow!" I yelled. "Tell her to dig us an escape hole."

Fatima was under the truck like a shot.

I turned my attention to the dashboard. A blast hit the passenger side door.

The GPS was built in. I pulled a screwdriver from my pocket and jammed it between the screen and plastic casing. I groaned as I tried to force it loose. I also didn't want to break it.

Fatima's head peered through the opening beside me. "Help me," I said.

She climbed in just as Elena's voice came through the passenger side window. "We've got company."

There was a roar above us as a ship approached,

rotors whirring. Red lights flashed. Elena began firing upward, one of her blast's hitting the mark. There was a sickening squeal and then more blasts hit the ground around us.

"We gotta go," Fatima said.

I continued leaning on the screwdriver. "We can't leave without this. I just don't want to bust it."

"I know," she said. She pulled a small blaster out of her sweater front and began firing at the dashboard. I held my hands up to shield my face from the bits of hot plastic that started flying around the cab.

"Okay, it's loose," Fatima said as more blasts shook the truck.

I lowered my hands. She had shot a square around the screen of the GPS, loosening a huge chunk of the dashboard.

I grabbed one end and Fatima held on to the other. Together we heaved it out, sending sparks flying as the wires snapped and ripped.

"Got it!" I yelled as loudly as I could.

Fatima kicked the door open and we slid out just as a blast tore through the front window, setting the cab on fire.

"Oooof!" I landed on the ground with a thud, still holding our prize.

"Quick, over here." It was Elena, under the truck, her head sticking out of a hole. "Thatcher isn't the only one who can use this trick." She disappeared.

Fatima and I got down on our hands and knees and crawled over, pushing the slab ahead of us. Elena popped up and grabbed it and then disappeared again. There were more blasts and then the sounds of footsteps. The last two things I saw as I slid down the hole were the pitch-black boots of about ten soldiers and the blue streak of the bomb Elena had thrown past my face, out of the hole, and under the truck.

Chapter Thirty
Rest Stop

"You have done some stupid things, Elena," I said as we sped away into the darkness underground. "But that was the stupidest."

"Agreed," Fatima said. "Plan B stands for bull . . ."

I coughed.

Elena inclined her head and stared at the GPS sitting on my lap. "I think you mean the *awesomest*."

"That's not even a word," Fatima said.

"The wires are all shot!" I said. "This is now the most useless paperweight in the history of . . . paperweights!"

Elena smiled. "We don't need the hardware. We just need the screen."

I opened my mouth to say something about how I

almost died for a stupid TV set, then I shut it. She was right. This was all we needed. Once we swapped it out for the old one, we could figure out where we were.

"Fine," I said. "Awesome."

"Thanks, Fearless," she said. "And since we could figure from the setting sun that we were facing north when we escaped, we are heading in, generally, the right direction. Right, Mandeep?"

"Right you are, General," Mandeep said. For the first time in days, she was grinning. Our little mission had yielded more than just some way to find our bearings. It felt good to do something dangerous again. Even Fatima gave a begrudging grin.

"Awesom*est*," I said. Although I couldn't shake the feeling that Elena's plan B had been plan A all along. "Did you get your battle fix up there?" I asked.

Elena just smiled and closed her eyes, hugging her blaster like a teddy bear. "Wake me up when we get there."

"Get where?"

Mandeep sped up and angled us more steeply downward. "Anywhere safe," she said.

"Anywhere safe" turned out to be a natural cavern at least a mile belowground. There was no sign anyone had ever been there besides us. We hit it accidentally but then decided it was a perfect place to do some repairs and grab some sleep.

Fatima and I busied ourselves chipping and cutting the remains of the dashboard off the new screen. We were being as careful as possible . . . and that was taking longer than I wanted.

"Well, that was a rush," Fatima said as she used a knife to scrape bits of melted plastic off the contacts at the back.

"Yeah," I agreed. "Between you and me, I think Elena enjoys that stuff a little too much."

"No, I don't," Elena called from the other side of the room. "I enjoy just as much as I need to."

I rolled my eyes. Fatima gave a short laugh. "I wonder what the news reports will make of that one. 'Grinder rebels attack greasy spoon.'"

Fatima chuckled.

"'Brave citizens fight back against terrorists using napkins and deep-fried schnitzel,'" I said.

I thought about what Beca had said about the risks of trying to contact someone out of the blue. Dozens of people had seen us trying to cross the road, trying to get into the truck. Not one had either recognized us or lifted a finger to help us.

"'Grinder attack. Child soldiers,'" I said, not laughing anymore.

"Yeah. If people weren't looking out for a digger full of rebels before, they sure are now," Fatima agreed.

"No kidding."

"Finished," Fatima said. She held up the cleaned screen and looked at it from all sides. "We should be able to get it to work."

She handed it to me. I walked over to the digger. Elena had removed the old screen and the hole in the dashboard looked roughly the same size.

I connected the wires and slid the screen into place. It fit, more or less, and I used some tape to cover the seams and hold it in place.

"It might jiggle a bit," I said. "But it should work."

Elena wiped her hands on her pant legs and leaned into the cockpit. "Now or never," she said.

I reached down and flipped on the power. The screen lit up. A grid of green lines showed our relative position. We were miles away from the next safe spot. Hundreds of miles.

I slumped back in the seat. "Great," I said, sarcastically.

"It is great," Elena said with a smile.

"Seriously? How?"

"Thatcher wasn't expecting us anywhere near that diner or whatever town that was."

"How do you figure that?"

"Those rotors you heard were from a surveillance drone. Armed but pretty easy to pick off with one shot."

I remembered the whir and then the high-pitched squeal as the drone had crashed to the ground.

"That means there was a base close by, but not one Thatcher had bothered to reinforce."

"How to do you figure that?" Fatima asked.

"C'mon. We attack that truck with multiple blasts and the only troops who show up are a drone and a tiny security patrol in a van? Nope. If Thatcher had been expecting us anywhere near that place, an attack on a Melming Mining truck would have brought a faster, and bigger, counterattack."

"But *now* he'll start looking there."

"And nearby," Fatima said. "But we've created a false trail."

Elena nodded. "Just because it was an accident doesn't mean it's not useful."

I turned off the digger. "Of course, the bad news is that we are that much farther away from where we're supposed to be. And who knows if it'll still be there." I yawned, despite myself.

"I'll start driving," Elena said. "You three can get some sleep in the cockpit."

"No," I said. "Let's all get some sleep. I have a feeling tomorrow is going to be the beginning of the end."

Elena opened her mouth to say something.

"That's an order," I said. Then I lay down on the seat and within seconds fell fast asleep.

Chapter Thirty-One
Target

We raced toward our goal, whatever it was. The coordinates were at the end of a fairly straight route that kept us away from water and well underground. We could risk going fast, and we needed to.

"Do you think it will still be safe there?" Mandeep asked.

"No idea," I said. I tapped the blaster on my lap. "I hope so."

Mandeep nodded but didn't say anything. She had a blaster on her lap too. We all did.

"We probably forced Thatcher's hand with that attack," Elena said. "He can't risk us pulling something like that again."

"Public and way out in the open," Fatima said.

"He'll be looking for us a little more eagerly now," Elena said with a hint of a smile.

"I suspect this was also part of your plan B?" I said.

"Sometimes the rabbit wants the fox to show itself."

"I have no idea what that means."

Elena smiled again and shrugged. "You can't deny that we needed the screen from that truck."

I watched the dot that represented our digger moving across the monitor screen. "True."

"That's all that matters."

We drove on silently after that.

To be honest, part of me was also happy that we had pushed things to the brink . . . not that I was going to tell Elena that. But a sense of calm had somehow come over all four of us.

We'd become accustomed to fighting, I realized. And good at it. I felt a mixture of sadness and a strange kind of elation at the thought.

"Almost there," Elena said, shaking me from my thoughts. She slowed the digger. I placed my hand on the trigger of the blaster and got ready for whatever was going to meet us.

The nose cone of the digger broke through into an empty space and shut off. Elena stopped, then backed up. She turned on the front camera. There was nothing in front of us but empty space. Of course, Beca's cave had looked much the same, and we'd stumbled into restraining cables.

Elena opened the cockpit but kept the engine running. "I'll go take a look," she said. "Chris. Get everyone out of here fast if you see anything suspicious."

"Not without you," I said.

"If Thatcher's troops are in there, you won't have that choice," she said ominously. She slipped out of the digger and slid down the side, her blaster aimed chest-high in front of her.

I got behind the wheel and prepared to drive forward, or backward, depending on what happened. The cockpit lid closed with a click.

Elena stopped at the mouth of the hole and peered inside. Her headlamp reflected off a wall of rock about forty feet on the other side. The room was large and dark. She looked up, down, and around before lifting her hand up and pointing at herself, then gesturing forward toward the hole. I held my breath as she disappeared into the shadows.

I inched the digger forward. There was the occasional flash of light as Elena continued sweeping the room with her headlamp. I sat tensely, my fingers braced on the wheel, my foot poised over the power pedal.

Elena's headlamp swung right at me and she turned it on and off. There were no restraining cords. No blinding lights. Nothing at all. I exhaled and drove inside.

Elena walked up and tapped on the window.

"It seems to be empty," she said. "No phone. No bombs or trip wires that I can see. It looks completely abandoned." The digger engine continued to hum.

"Maybe they left when we didn't show up on time," Fatima said. "Moved on."

"Beca said they don't like to linger," Mandeep agreed.

Fatima sighed. "So I guess we wait for them to contact us with some new coordinates? But we should move."

"I'm sick of moving," Elena said. She continued scanning the room, her headlamp reflecting off nothing but bare rock. When she looked up, her light only just reached the high ceiling.

"So what's your plan B here?" I said.

She pointed at the ceiling. "We have company. I'm going to say hello."

"I thought you said it was abandoned."

"Remember that hidden camera trick we used on Thatcher back on Perses?"

I nodded.

Elena took a step back and aimed her blaster upward,

peering through the sight. "I said it *looks* completely abandoned. I didn't say it was."

I looked up but couldn't see anything.

She moved the barrel of the blaster back and forth like a metronome before stopping. She stood still, the light from her helmet like a faint spotlight on the target.

"Funny that there's one shiny speck of ore in just one spot on the ceiling when there's none on an entire half-mile of exposed wall."

I looked at the ceiling. She was right. There was just the tiniest reflection. One tiny star in a void of blackish-gray.

"Hello," she said, moving her light and blaster just a fraction to the left of the dot. Then she fired. The blast sent a chunk of rock crashing to the floor not more than a foot away from us. She waited for the dust to clear, then walked over, knelt down, and began picking through the shattered stone. She grabbed something small and held it up in the glow of her headlamp. It was a tiny metal box with the melted remains of wire sticking out the sides.

"Now what?" I said.

Elena looked back at the room. "We wait."

"For what?"

"For whoever shows up first."

Chapter Thirty-Two

Hello

Every drip of moisture, every tiny shifting of the rock, sent shivers up my spine. We were all standing on the seat of the digger, the cockpit open, our blasters ready to fire up, down, sideways . . . wherever our friends, or enemies, arrived from.

"What are they waiting for?" Mandeep said in a hushed voice, as if any echo might trigger an attack.

Elena didn't bother whispering. "They want to make sure they don't get shot, if they are grinders, or that they can shoot us first, if they are Thatcher's goons." The word "goons" came back at us from all sides of the cavern.

"Can we not do that?" I said.

"They know we're here," Elena said, in a slightly lower voice. "There's no tactical advantage in not being able to hear each other clearly."

"Shhhhh," Fatima said. "Someone is coming."

We froze, straining to hear.

A few moments later some loose stones on the floor began to shake and dance.

A hum grew in the rock wall to our left. Elena held up her weapon and aimed it.

"Aim at the walls," she said, pointing. "We have no idea how many of them are here, or if they are going to come at us from all sides."

The hum got louder by the second, still from just the one wall. Then all of a sudden, it stopped. A small trickle of dust fell slowly from partway up the wall to the floor.

"Nose cone," I said. "Just barely broke through."

"Masks on," Elena said. "Chris first."

I lowered my blaster and quickly covered my face. I tightened the straps, then put on my helmet, resumed aiming my blaster, and signaled for Fatima to go next.

I watched the tiny hole, waiting for some sign that gas was being pumped in to knock us unconscious or kill us. But the dust in my headlamp seemed relatively still, floating rather than agitated.

Then a light shot out like a laser, reflecting off the far wall.

"Get down," Elena said, her voice only slightly muffled by the mask.

"Wait!" Mandeep called, pointing. "The light. It's flicking on and off."

She was right, and it was no arbitrary pattern. Pavel had taught me some Morse code when we'd been cooped up in the radio room on Perses waiting for an answer to the beacon.

I was no expert, but I could make out these letters easily. I'd seen them before.

```
....  .  ._..  ._..  _ _ _
....  .  ._..  ._..  _ _ _
....  .  ._..  ._..  _ _ _
....  .  ._..  ._..  _ _ _
```

H.E.L.L.O.
H.E.L.L.O.
H.E.L.L.O.
H.E.L.L.O.

"The Oracle," I said. "She's here."

Elena stopped moving. I pointed my headlamp at the

wall next to the blinking light and answered "Hello," using the same pattern. The blinking stopped and the hidden digger began burrowing through the rock.

"Keep your guns up and ready to fire," Elena said. "And keep an eye on the rest of the cave."

The digger cut through the wall slowly until the cockpit emerged. Then it stopped. It was a normal mining digger, old and battered. No guns that we could see. The cockpit lid opened.

A woman in a dark-gray uniform stood up in the seat, her arms raised high to show she was unarmed. Her hair was gray, and her eyes were a piercing blue. She looked familiar, although I was sure we had never met. Fatima kept scanning the other walls. "Nothing coming," she said, relaxing slightly.

"Hello," the woman said, then she smiled, her arms remaining above her head. That voice. The voice that had spoken to us on the transport as we approached Earth.

I lowered my gun and jumped down from our digger. Elena kept her blaster raised as I made my way over.

"Oracle?" I said.

The woman nodded. "But my real name is Tatiana. Tatiana Melming."

Chapter Thirty-Three
Answers

I stood completely still as her voice, her name, bounced off the walls. Of course. *Of course.*

"You're his granddaughter," I said.

"Yes. And his only ally at Melming Mining, until my recent . . . involuntary retirement." She gave a short laugh. "But seeing you here, alive, makes me hope that sacrifice was worth it."

There was a series of noises from our digger as Fatima and Mandeep lowered their weapons. The Oracle lowered her arms. "May I join you?" she asked.

She slipped down the side of her machine, wincing in obvious pain. Her right leg was covered in bandages. She took a moment to straighten up and saw me staring.

"My *retirement*, after I was discovered by Thatcher, was not as clean an escape as I would have liked. Most of the bones in my leg are broken, but I can get around okay. He hasn't caught me . . . yet."

The others joined us.

"We need some answers," Elena said.

The Oracle nodded. "You deserve many." She leaned against the side of her digger and lowered herself down until she was sitting on the ground. She gave a sigh and straightened out her leg. "That's better. Now, where to begin."

"Let's start with how you ended up helping us," Mandeep said.

"I am, as Christopher said, Hans Melming's granddaughter."

"In line for the top job?" Elena said, with more than a tinge of skepticism. More than once she'd wondered if the Oracle had used us to take out Thatcher for her.

"No," Tatiana said. "It's a reasonable suspicion, but no. I was a scientist, like my grandfather. Though not a genius like he was . . . is." She paused for a moment before resuming. "I was once a member of the communications team. We designed satellites, receivers, wave-form relays. And something elegant called the Interface, and . . ."

"Emergency beacons," Fatima said.

The Oracle smiled. "Just one. But that is getting ahead of the story by a few years. Melming Mining, when it began, was a noble venture. It was set up to help save the Earth. The Great Mission *was* meant to be great."

"But you were still using grinders," Fatima said. "So even at the beginning it was compromised."

"Yes. Most mining companies were."

"That's not an excuse," Fatima said.

"No. It isn't. And it is a guilt and shame we must accept. And when the world governments consolidated everything under the Melming umbrella, we should have eradicated the practice. Perhaps that was the beginning of the cancer that soon spread through the company."

"Thatcher," I said.

"Before Thatcher. Already, even at the start, there was greed alongside the more noble aspirations of my grandfather. He was a scientist, not a businessman or a politician. So he left the running of the company to others. They began to increase the number of grinders. Your father, Christopher, was part of this first escalation, in preparation for the Great Mission."

I thought of the double-*M* tattoo he'd tried to keep hidden from me. My hand reflexively went to the ink on my own arm. He was probably no older than me when he was first sent to the mines.

The Oracle continued. "These managers consolidated more and more power. They began to promote
their supporters and actively suppress anyone who
questioned their authority. They told my grandfather
one story, while secretly planning the plunder of Perses
for their own profit."

"Your grandfather never suspected?"

"It was all well hidden, in the beginning. They were
just building a network of allies, putting them in positions of authority, waiting for their moment to seize
control."

"Jimmi's dad," Elena said.

The Oracle nodded. "While working on company
transmissions, I uncovered secret coded messages coming through on a hidden frequency. I traced the origins.
They were being sent and received from within the
company." She sighed. "I tried to tell my grandfather.
But he didn't believe me. Everything seemed so orderly.
If he had acted then, perhaps . . ." She closed her eyes
for a second and took a deep breath. "In any case, I
continued to monitor the transmissions. I cracked their
code and began to keep a file of what was being talked
about and who was talking."

"That's when you heard Thatcher planning his attack
on the first cargo ships," Elena said.

"He was never brazen or stupid enough to say exactly what his plans were, even over his own secure lines. But he knew full well when the first shipments would be arriving. And he knew that the general in charge, the general he blamed for the attack, was a former grinder. Once news of the attack reached us at headquarters, I knew what had really happened."

"Did you say anything?"

She shook her head. "There were too many people in the hierarchy who cheered his victory. An open revolt was suicide. Instead, I bided my time and looked for my own allies. There were only a few, mostly in my sector. But they helped me establish a series of relays, satellites, and frequencies."

"That's how you were able to reach us on the transport," Elena said.

"It was dangerous. Each time I broadcast from a relay point, it was compromised—quickly found and destroyed by Thatcher's troops. Eventually they closed in." She glanced down at her leg, rubbing it and wincing.

"So what about the beacon?" Fatima asked.

"When the personnel were named for the Great Mission, a few stood out. Your parents, Christopher and Elena, were not sent just because of their skill. They were exiled."

"Exiled? For what?"

"Your parents had been part of secret meetings here on Earth, along with many others, including Pavel's mother."

His mother. The radio telecommunications expert. "She worked with you?" I said.

"It was very hard for her to keep her real work quiet. Especially with her husband being such a . . . It doesn't matter anymore."

"Secret meetings?" Mandeep asked.

"Grinder meetings. They talked of organizing, making public demands for their freedom. Nothing dangerous or remotely rebellious, at first. Some of us from inside Melming Mining were also there. But even the hint of an organized opposition sent a chill through the company. So they shipped out the lead dissidents. We feared that wouldn't be the end of it. I approached your father, Chris. We arranged to have a beacon sent, in parts, along with other supplies. Assembled, it would have been discovered. In small parts, it was easy to send undetected."

"My mother's handwriting was part of the reassembly," I said, in a whisper. "They'd pieced it together, without the company knowing, in their off hours under the planet's core."

"I am sorry that we didn't do more to prevent this. I never truly believed Thatcher was capable of such depths of evil. Once the beacon was destroyed . . . I was forced into hiding, and I have been working with the rebels ever since. I have not risked contacting my grandfather again."

She began to shake and I realized she was crying. "I am so sorry. This should never have happened."

"Do you still trust your grandfather?" I said.

Elena scoffed. "Chris, c'mon. You heard her. He's done nothing to stop . . ." I held up a hand to quiet her.

"Do you trust him?"

She raised her head, jutting her chin proudly in the air. She stole a glance at the far wall of the room, then swung her eyes back on mine—intense, as if she were boring a hole right through me.

"I have this memory of him. I was at his winter home, deep in the woods of Norway. It was breakfast. The clock struck eight, and I heard his voice coming from his den. It was a beautiful room. Lined with oak. Overlooking the lake. I peered inside. He was talking, loudly, but there seemed to be no one else there.

"I tiptoed over to his desk and crawled by the feet of his chair. He saw me and gave a tiny smile but never stopped his phantom conversation. His right hand was pressing a button underneath his desk. He was announcing the Great Mission. He articulated it so clearly. The importance. The elegance. A mission that would save the Earth and would inspire the people of the world. He believed it in the very bottom of his soul."

I nodded. "I know that speech. We studied it in school, watched videos of the address. I can even remember the oak-paneled room, the sparkling water reflecting in the background."

The Oracle kept her eyes locked on mine. "I could hear the same speech just a few moments later coming from the radio in the breakfast room. I had left the door open. He motioned for me to close it, quickly. He later said the echo made it hard for him to concentrate. I crawled over and closed the door and he continued, ending with a vow to do everything possible to keep the Great Mission from failure, including pledging his own life.

"Afterward, he released the button and the transmission ended. He said I could stand. That no one could see me. 'The Interface,' he said. 'Tell no one.' And I haven't told a soul. Until this moment."

She told me more. About tea and marmalade and details that seemed so mundane I almost ignored them. But she continued to stare at me, boring into me with her eyes, willing me to pay attention. "Remember this story."

I just stared back, confused. "But . . ."

Before I could say another word, Fatima stood up like a shot. She raised her blaster.

"We've got company."

Chapter Thirty-Four
Goodbye

The cave shook like an earthquake.

"Everybody move!" Elena yelled. She and Fatima raised their blasters and hurried back to our digger. The hum grew louder by the second and seemed to be coming from everywhere.

"Chris! Mandeep!" Fatima yelled.

Mandeep looked down at the Oracle's leg, then up at me. I saw what she saw. The Oracle's wound was bleeding, a lot.

"This just happened, didn't it?" Mandeep asked.

"Yes. This morning. I thought I had lost them, but they must have followed. I'm sorry," said the Oracle. She tried to move and her face contorted in pain. "Go. I can stand up on my own."

Even I could tell she was lying.

"I've got her," Mandeep said. "Get back to the digger."

"No," said the Oracle. "I'll be fine."

The walls were now shedding loose stones and dirt.

Mandeep shot me a look. "Go," she mouthed.

But I had one more thing to ask the Oracle.

"Where's the next safe house?"

"Nowhere is safe anymore," she said. Then she pulled an ancient phone out of her chest pocket, turned on the power, and handed it to me. "The Interface. Remember."

Mandeep lifted the Oracle up and they shuffled toward the cockpit of her digger.

I ran. The noise was now almost deafening. The phone buzzed in my hand and I stole a look at the screen.

684954

16 . . .

There were more numbers, but I never saw them.

There was a sound like a thunderclap, and a huge slab of rock crashed to the floor. The force knocked me over. As I fell, the phone slipped out of my hand and spun across the floor.

"CHRIS!" Elena's voice boomed over the noise. I scrambled to my feet just as an enormous wheel of jagged teeth gnawed through the wall in front of me, ripping and tearing at the rock, which collapsed in bigger and bigger chunks. Stones flew off it like bullets.

I had never seen an excavator at work before and it was terrifying. I was staring into the mouth of a giant beast. The phone was right in front, flopping on the ground like a fish out of water. I lunged for it but something stopped me, suspended me in midair. I was immediately yanked backward, choking.

"Leave the phone." It was Fatima's voice in my ear. I could feel her strong hand on the collar of my uniform. Elena had driven right next to me and Fatima had leaned down to grab me.

The excavator moved toward us. The phone, caught in the wheel, hit a tooth and then spun off into the darkness. If Fatima hadn't caught me, I'd have been killed. She pulled me up toward the cockpit as Elena swerved to avoid the gnashing teeth. I swung in the air like a rag doll, my back sliding along the hull of the digger, my feet swaying just inches from the deadly teeth.

Fatima grunted as she struggled to haul me into the

digger. I grabbed one of her hands and pulled. With a heave, she swung me up and over the side.

"Finally!" Elena yelled. She closed the cockpit lid and began speeding down the length of the cave.

"Where's Mandeep?" I said.

"On the other side of that." Elena pointed at a wall of rubble in the middle of the cave.

"We saw you trying to do some ninja heroics with the phone and figured we'd better save you first."

"Thanks," I said.

"No problem."

I looked back. The excavator was cutting crazily behind us, but now that it was in the open space of the cave, it moved more slowly and fell back as we sped forward.

Elena hit the rockslide and ignited the disrupter. Just as it had done on Perses, the energy burst blew a hole in the rubble pile. Rocks flew off in all directions. One huge piece dinged off the ceiling and narrowly missed smashing our own hull. But the maneuver had cleared a path through the pile. Elena gunned the engine.

Just ahead of us I could see the Oracle, her cockpit lid still open, driving toward us. Mandeep was standing on the seat, firing blaster shots. In seconds I saw the reason. Another excavator had broken through behind them.

Our radio crackled to life. "Stop running."

Thatcher's voice.

Was he here? My skin crawled as he spoke again.

"You are trapped, surrounded. There are excavators and diggers behind all the remaining walls. It's over. Surrender." I could hear the sneer in his voice.

Another excavator broke through to our left. Elena slammed on the brakes and swerved to avoid it. Its teeth continued to spin and gnaw as it moved toward us.

"These aren't here to take us prisoner," Elena said. "This is it."

The excavators continued to bear down on us. Another broke through to the right, forcing us to swerve again.

In just seconds we would be surrounded.

Elena flicked on the radio. "Mandeep. Evasive action!" She slammed our digger in reverse and then spun around.

The gap between the excavators was getting smaller and smaller, like the walls of a room closing in, ready-ing to crush us. Elena shot forward, slipping through a crack barely larger than our machine. The teeth of the cutterheads sliced the air just a fraction of an inch from our hull.

We'd made it through. Elena slammed on the brakes and turned.

Mandeep and the Oracle were trapped. The gap had

shrunk too much. The Oracle was trying to spin the digger, desperate for any opening she could find, but the machines continued to close in. Then she stopped, the cockpit visible in a crack of light between two excavators. She and Mandeep faced us and I could see them looking from side to side, panicked. Then Mandeep's eyes met mine. She became calm. She saluted. Then the bulk of the excavators closed the gap, blocking them from view.

Elena and Fatima yelled in anger, but I couldn't hear the words. I was too shocked to register anything. Elena opened the cockpit and stood on the seat, firing at the excavators, but they marched forward, unrelenting.

Then there was the sound of more digging, not in front of us but from the remains of the walls behind us.

"We have to go," I said steadily. "We have to get out of here."

Elena swung her head and glared at me, hyperventilating . . . and furious. But she lowered her blaster and slammed herself back down on the seat. Fatima kept her eyes on the back of the excavators as she collapsed next to me. The cockpit lid lowered. But we could still hear the horrible screech as the teeth of the excavators began ripping through metal.

Elena pounded her fists on the wheel but turned us

away to escape into the rock. The last thing I saw before we broke into the wall was the blue flash of a disrupter being fired.

Trapped into the shrinking space between the swirling teeth, the disrupter wouldn't shut off. The digger was now a bomb. Only someone who'd been with us on Perses would know that. The telltale squeal rose above the noise of the chaos.

Then the entire cave exploded behind us and the tunnel we'd just made collapsed in a rain of shattered rock.

Chapter Thirty-Five

Latitude

Thatcher had said there were diggers waiting in the rock, but by some miracle we avoided them. Or maybe it wasn't a miracle. Maybe it was Mandeep. The explosion Mandeep had triggered took out whatever else was in that room, and a huge chunk of rock surrounding it. Somehow we'd avoided that too.

We were flying at top speed away from the cave, not daring to speak.

But I knew we didn't have time to grieve for Mandeep or the Oracle. Thatcher had known we were coming. He'd known the Oracle was meeting us. We'd been late getting to the rendezvous point. She'd waited. That had given him time to track her, locate her, and find us.

We'd escaped. But he must have guessed where she'd send us. To see Hans Melming.

Thatcher would be waiting.

We would have to be ready.

I took a deep breath.

"We have to figure out a plan fast," I said, wiping my nose.

"Agreed. Mourning is a luxury right now," Elena said, even though her own voice wavered. "We have to *end* this."

"Did the Oracle say where to head next, Chris?" Fatima said.

"Norway. Melming. But the coordinates were on that phone. I only saw half of them before I dropped the stupid thing." I cursed. If I'd only kept hold of the phone, stashed it in my pocket to check later, Mandeep and the Oracle might be alive. Elena could have gone to help them instead of having to save my useless butt.

"We wouldn't have reached them any sooner," Elena said softly, guessing my thoughts for the hundredth time. She and Fatima both looked at me. "There was nothing we could have done."

"Run through the timeline in your head. You know it's true," Fatima said.

A lump rose in my throat. "Fine. We can't waste any time on this now."

The dashboard map showed that we were heading down, and north.

"Finding Melming will be like finding a needle in a haystack," Elena said.

"I've always thought that was a dumb analogy," Fatima said. "Just keep sticking your hand in there until something stabs you. Easy."

"Nice. A much better analogy. Getting stabbed," Elena said.

They continued to argue, but it was just to blow off some steam, so I let them. It was better than a silence that we would only fill with sorrow.

I thought back to the story the Oracle had told me. She'd never wavered in her gaze. She clearly wanted me to remember every detail. It was more than a memory. It was filled with clues that could help us formulate a plan. She must have suspected Thatcher could hear, so she hadn't given specific instructions.

I interrupted the fight. "She said it was deep in the woods. Near a lake. The first series of numbers were 684954 and, I think, the number 16. The first part must be 68 degrees latitude. The north pole is 90, so we work down toward the equator from that."

"So north," Elena said. "But we knew that already."

"The other four numbers and the 16 help us focus it in a bit more than that," I said.

"How much is 'a bit' when we're talking the Earth?" Elena said.

I scrolled north on the map. The line of latitude on the phone crossed hundreds of miles of Norwegian land, numerous mountains, fjords, and even the upper parts of Sweden and Finland. Almost all of it seemed to be near water and covered in trees.

Elena saw that too. "So we hit that line and do what? Start crisscrossing northern Norway until we hit a cabin with oak paneling?"

"We can't just pop up every ten feet with Thatcher waiting there to blast us," Fatima said.

"I know," I said. "I know. But if 16 represents the longitude, that helps us too."

I plugged in the 16, and it showed a location right in the middle of the Norwegian Sea.

"Anyone know how to swim?" Elena joked.

"No, it's good," I said.

"How?"

I drew an imaginary line with my finger along the gap between the 15th and 17th longitude lines. There was a lot of water but only one stretch of land, about twenty kilometers long.

I remembered the Oracle's story.

It was a beautiful room. Lined with oak. Overlooking the lake.

"Lake," I repeated. I zoomed in. There was a lot of water on the line but only one lake. A huge one. I pointed at it. "Bingo."

Elena looked skeptical. "That's a big lake. Melming's cottage could be anywhere on that thing."

"But it's there. And getting Melming to watch that video, to believe our story—it's the only real chance we have left."

"How do we even know Melming is still there?" Elena said.

"She wanted me to memorize every detail of her story. He was there. Why else describe it so precisely? She said he could be convinced. She said he believed in the Great Mission. We are all that is left of that mission. He'll be there. He'll listen."

"Why didn't she just tell you where this stupid place was?" Elena fumed.

"She was probably going to," Fatima said.

"She knew Thatcher had to be close," Elena said. "Maybe it was by listening to her radio?"

"Thatcher might have bugged the cave, but he didn't track anyone," I said.

"What do you mean?"

"Those excavators can't travel like diggers. They had to have been waiting nearby, ready to move in and kill Tatiana and anyone else who showed up."

"So he must have known about that cave for a while. And had people watching it," Fatima said.

I shook my head. "Not watching. Those excavators were robotic. No drivers. We must have triggered some sensor that made them operational. Thatcher's voice was weird too. Did you notice that?"

Elena nodded. "Younger. Stronger."

"He wasn't there. He would have named us. That was some kind of recording."

"The Oracle would never have come if she didn't think it was safe," Fatima said.

I agreed. "Thatcher might have a spy somewhere in the grinder rebellion. Someone told her the location would be safe, and then it wasn't."

Elena had another thought. "I dunno. I think she knew it wasn't safe but came to warn us as quickly as she could. She suspected she was being followed. She'd just been attacked."

I thought of how tentatively the Oracle had entered

the cave, signaling with code rather than driving right in. How she'd sped there after escaping Thatcher's troops, and her relief when she saw we were there alone. Elena was right. Somehow the Oracle knew we were in danger, so she'd risked her own life to warn us.

We *were* alive, but she and Mandeep had paid the ultimate price for our freedom.

"Do you think Thatcher knows where we're headed now?" Fatima asked.

"We have to assume that he does."

Elena pointed at the map. "Find me a direct route underground and we'll go as fast as we can. We either get there first . . ."

". . . Or arrive ready to fight whoever does."

Elena nodded and I began plugging in the coordinates.

Fatima reached under the seat and pulled out Mandeep's backpack. She stared at it for a good minute, motionless, before sliding it back underneath and grabbing her own. She opened it silently and passed us some chocolate bars and drinks.

"Eat," she said. "We're going to need the energy."

Chapter Thirty-Six

Surfacing

Thatcher's voice woke me from a deep sleep. "Despite increased security measures, grinder attacks have increased."

I was in our cockpit. We were stopped. Fatima was snoring loudly.

Elena was leaning on the steering wheel, staring straight ahead, the light from the console giving her face an eerie glow. Her lips were set, eyes narrowed.

"Did I just hear Thatcher?"

Elena nodded. "He's giving some kind of speech." She turned up the radio slightly and Thatcher's voice returned.

"There is now a Global Code Red situation. All citizens

are ordered to stay alert. Be on the lookout for anyone with grinder markings. Notify authorities of any suspicious behavior. Action will be taken. Deadly force if necessary. Just today we uncovered and neutralized a cell of grinder terrorists."

He paused for effect. No doubt listeners around the globe were shaking in fear at Thatcher's latest warning of immediate danger.

"How are we hearing this?"

Elena pointed up. "We're close to the surface. We need to repower."

Thatcher gave a slight cough. This was his new voice again, scratchy. I could almost see his face, smug and scarred.

"We have reason to believe these are the same rebels who coordinated the recent, and fatal, attacks on the Great Mission on Perses."

Elena gave a low growl.

"As you know, my troops and I recently returned from Perses after successfully quashing the uprising there. Many died to save our way of life here on Earth. Melming's Great Mission will continue. I have dispatched a troop of soldiers back to the colony to begin reestablishing the infrastructure."

"Darcy!" I gasped.

"A clean slate will mean a new dawn for the Earth and all humankind. And I will wipe the dirt from our world clean."

For the first time, I heard the cheers. This wasn't just a speech but a rally of some kind. The crowd began chanting Thatcher's name over and over.

"I'm not dreaming this, am I?" I asked Elena.

"Nightmare, yes. Sleeping? No."

Thatcher continued. *"These grinder rebels have no respect for human life. They have infiltrated our society in order to destroy it from within. Even the highest levels of Melming Mining have been compromised. Anyone seen with an M or double-M tattoo should immediately be turned over to the authorities."*

I couldn't suppress a shocked laugh. The irony of his lies was too much. But he had one more.

"I have seen with my own eyes how these grinders will stop at nothing, even killing children to get what they want."

The crowd murmured angrily. Was he showing them something?

"Yes. These are horrible images of the children of Perses. All of them killed in the attacks. Grinders did this

there, and they want to continue that brutality here."

I wanted to throw up. Thatcher was the murderer. And he was using images of his own massacre to justify even more horrors.

"These images must be seen. Rest assured that we are closing in on the few remaining cells. We will find them. We will destroy them. And with your help, and cooperation, we will be victorious."

The crowd began chanting his name again.

Elena angrily switched off the radio. "We have to move faster."

"Agreed. That speech must be live. I'm sure he was talking about the Oracle when he made that comment about the 'highest levels of Melming Mining.' Any idea where he was?"

"Oslo. Melming HQ. He said it near the beginning."

A thought occurred to me. "Maybe he thinks that's where we're headed. HQ."

"And he's letting us know he's already there by giving this speech. He's daring us to attack . . ."

" . . . Or scaring us off," I said. "But we aren't going to Melming HQ. We're going to Melming himself. If he's guessed wrong, it might buy us some time to look around the lake."

"Some time, but not much. Still, if that's true, we'll take it," Elena said. She turned the digger back on and started driving up.

We broke through the surface.

The sunlight was so bright we had to shield our eyes. That was good news.

Fatima woke up and blinked against the sunlight. "Pit stop?"

"Yup," Elena said.

Luck was on our side. We'd surfaced in the middle of a farmer's field.

Tall shafts of wheat surrounded us, keeping us hidden, at least from anyone on land.

Elena leaped out of the digger. "We have to recharge the batteries. But the good news is that should give us enough power to get to Melming without surfacing again."

I ran the calculations in my head. Our plan was to dig east and then north before turning back south to the coordinates the Oracle had given us. A distance of about four thousand kilometers, or about three days of digging at top speed.

"How is that possible? We'll have to stop at least once more, won't we?"

Elena shook her head as she began spreading the solar panel on the hull. "No. We're going that way." She pointed straight north. "The shortest distance between two points is always a straight line."

"But that takes us . . ."

"Under a lot of water. Hope you packed your swimsuits."

Chapter Thirty-Seven
Submarine

The rock around us was still rock, but it felt different. I couldn't shake the feeling that the water was pressing down on top of me, that the rock was saturated and dripping wet, a constant threat. Every ting on our windshield was a drip of water signaling our doom.

Elena wasn't exactly calming.

"Relax. It's not like we're going under the ocean. This is just a short plunge."

"Don't say *plunge*."

"I'm kidding. The channel between here and Norway is like, maybe, a mile deep. We're further down than that."

But all I heard was *maybe*.

I knew it was crazy, but the air in the digger suddenly felt clammy, damp.

All we needed to do was nick the bottom of the channel and water would flood the tunnel. We'd either be drowned or crushed by the pressure. In a weird way, it was like being on the transport in space, surrounded by an unfeeling and deadly vacuum.

But Elena was right. This path would save us hours of driving, and we were going to need every small advantage we could get if we were going to reach Melming before Thatcher guessed exactly what we were up to. It was time for risks.

"How much longer?" I asked.

Fatima was still, but her eyes darted around constantly. "Another twenty minutes."

Elena dipped down slightly, which I appreciated, and we continued digging almost straight north.

And then we hit it.

One second we were burning through rock. The next, we lurched to a stop, surrounded by water. The disrupter continued to burn, churning the water around us, boiling it and infusing it with an electric-blue glow. We began to sink, the water around us bubbling furiously, the cockpit getting increasingly hot.

"Shut it off!" I yelled.

Elena scrambled to find the switch while the digger continued to drop.

A burst of water shot through the vent, spraying our faces. The air intakes, designed to keep out rock and dirt, were clearly never meant to be exposed to water.

Salt stung my eyes.

I pushed my hand through the fountain and switched off the life support. We were now falling in complete darkness. "We've got about one minute of oxygen," I said.

"On it," came Fatima's voice. She flicked on her headlamp, got down on the floor, and grabbed the masks Beca had given us days before.

"These are low on air," she said, handing them up. "Stay calm."

Then she put hers on. Staying calm was not easy.

The digger drifted down in the churning waters. With the engine and the oxygen shut off, we were dead in the water. My mind raced.

Elena lifted her mask. "Now what?"

The only answer I could give was to turn on the headlights. They barely lit the gloom around us. We were in an enormous metal shaft. The rusted and barnacled walls rose into darkness above and below. Bits of debris and tiny fish passed through the light like dust.

"It's some kind of abandoned oil shaft," Fatima said. "Dug way down into the earth below the bottom of the channel."

In our haste, we'd smashed right into it. So much for whatever luck had been with us.

Something caused a disturbance in the water and the digger shifted slightly to the left, tilting us almost upside down. We struggled to hold our spots on the seat without smashing into each other, which made us spin even more.

I lifted my mask. "I have an idea. Get ready to fire the disrupter."

Elena nodded.

I opened the trunk. Huge bubbles began floating out of it, all around us, but the force of the released air shot us forward toward the far wall.

Elena didn't need me to tell her what to do next. The instant our nose cone touched the metal, she fired the disrupter. The cone dug into the wall and burned through. We shot into the surrounding rock and began driving away at top speed.

One problem. The water was rushing after us. And our oxygen supply was quickly running out. We were all releasing way too much carbon dioxide into the cockpit.

Elena tried turning on the air intake, but a splash of

salty water ended that plan, and she quickly shut it off.

"We can't escape," she said, the words muffled by her mask. "There's no way to collapse the tunnel."

Fatima lifted her mask. "Up," she said.

Elena closed her eyes and pulled back on the steering column. We began to rise, the water still gushing after us.

I began to panic, knowing my heavy breaths were speeding up our suffocation but incapable of slowing them.

The lights of the dashboard began to swim in front of me, my head bobbing forward. I saw a sudden glimpse of my parents, back at the Blackout Bash, dancing and having fun. Then Elena was on the dance floor, waving for me to join her. I reached out.

Then everything turned red.

Chapter Thirty-Eight
Gasp

The red quickly turned to brilliant sunshine. I struggled to take a breath, the mask sitting loosely on my face. I ripped it off, the air still thick and useless. I felt like I was drowning.

Drowning in sunlight?

We were on the surface. Sights and sounds came at me all at once. The drill of the digger was still running. We were moving. People were yelling.

I sat up straight. We were in the middle of a wide-open field, with the sun high in the sky. People, farm workers as far as I could tell, were running away from us into the nearby trees. At least one held a hand to her ear, calling someone.

I yelled a curse. The effort burned my throat. The air inside the digger was turning toxic.

I reached down and shut off the engine, then opened the lid of the cockpit. It opened a crack, then stuck.

Elena and Fatima lay motionless against the back of the seat. I ripped their masks off and jammed my own face against the open lid, gasping for air.

Elena stirred next to me, groaning as the precious oxygen filled her lungs.

"Where are we?"

I looked down at the console. Dead.

"On land," I croaked. "And sitting ducks."

"On it."

Elena was up like a shot. She saw the cockpit lid barely open and slid on her back, feet raised. She kicked at the hinge until it opened enough for her to climb out.

Fatima, roused by the air and the noise, sat up straight.

"We out of the water?"

"Yes. I'm not sure how long we were moving for, but the battery is completely drained."

"Great," she said, rubbing her forehead. "And I have one heck of a headache."

I climbed out to join Elena.

She was pulling the soaking-wet solar panel out of

the back. She shook it violently and flung it over the hull.

"Luckily this was attached to the digger," she said. "The rest of the stuff—blasters, food, everything—got jettisoned when we opened the trunk back in that shaft."

"Sorry."

"We'd be dead if you hadn't done that. It was brilliant."

There was a gurgle and a whir from the hull. Fatima stuck her head over the side of the cockpit. Her hair was dripping and her face covered with water. "Air filtration system is clear now. But your butts are going to get a little wet."

Her head disappeared.

"See? Could be way worse," Elena said.

"Pretty sure Thatcher knows where we are. That's pretty bad."

"Not bad. It's good," Elena said.

"Are you nuts?"

She shrugged. "He knew we were going to Norway. If anything, this'll make him even more sure that we're heading for Oslo."

"In case you hadn't noticed, we're not heading anywhere right now."

She seemed unconcerned and even yawned as she leaned against the hull of the digger.

"This solar thing works super-fast, you may remember, and we don't need a full tank to make it to Melming."

"There must be troops on their way now. The woods over there are full of witnesses."

Elena glanced at the sky. "My guess, he's still not ready to attack us in the open."

"Why not?"

She pointed at the trees. "You've got a bunch of people over there who just saw a piece of space mining equipment burst out of the ground and charge at them. Exactly what Thatcher has been telling them to expect." She cupped her hands around her mouth and yelled, "Can anyone tell me how far to Oslo? Anyone?" Then she looked at me and winked.

"You think he's just going to sit at HQ and wait for us?"

"That's where he's strongest. He's got his troops ready and waiting. Shooting us out here finishes us off but leaves our bodies on the surface, with people around . . . That's not the long game."

"You think he *wants* an attack on Melming HQ?"

"A failed attack is perfect. Pure propaganda gold."

We were interrupted by the sound of an approaching helicopter, the rotors cutting through the air.

"Of course, I could be wrong."

Elena pulled a blaster from some hidden pocket of her overalls and knelt down on the ground, ready to fire.

"Chris!" Fatima called from the digger. She held up a blaster and tossed it to me. I got down on the ground next to Elena and wrapped my finger around the trigger.

The helicopter, blue-black, stopped at the edge of the field and hovered. I tensed, expecting a missile launch at any second.

"Surrender, grinder rebels," boomed a voice from the sky. "Put down your weapons."

"Power is at twenty-five percent," Fatima called.

The copter continued to hover. Ten seconds passed. It fired a missile. I shot at it but missed. I flung myself to the ground, expecting the worst, but the missile flew past us and exploded a few yards away.

I looked up. Elena hadn't budged. Hadn't fired.

"This is a show," Elena said. "They want us to attack. That's a drone. No humans on board."

"So what do we do?"

"I always wanted to be in show business," Elena said. She stood and yelled at the top of her lungs, "We're coming for you, Thatcher!"

Then she fired, the blast hitting the copter on top,

shearing the rotors straight off. One lodged in the trunk of a tree. The others flew into the ground like spears, sending plumes of dirt and grass flying into the air. The hull seemed to fall in slow-motion before crashing to the ground with a burst of fire.

"The lead on the six o'clock news," Elena said. She marched back to the solar panel, rolled it up, and shoved it back in the trunk.

"But didn't you just blow up whatever camera was on board?" I asked, getting to my feet and looking around for the next wave of copters, troops, or both.

"Don't look up. But listen."

I strained and heard it. The slight beating of a much smaller set of rotors far up above us.

"Filming the whole thing," I said. "So we've got eye-witnesses in the woods to back up some threats on the news. Just what Thatcher wants."

"Bingo," Elena said. "Now I suggest we get moving."

Chapter Thirty-Nine
Slowdown

We didn't encounter any more hidden tunnels or drone copters.

But we did make one more stop. I estimated how long it would have taken us to reach Melming HQ. If Thatcher was expecting us and we didn't show, I wanted to see if he'd tip his hand for his next move.

Elena dug close to the surface and we turned on the radio. What we heard both chilled us and cheered us.

We hadn't shown up, but others had.

"A bold attack today on Melming Mining Headquarters.

"Using diggers and trucks full of explosives, grinder rebels approached the security perimeter just before

dawn. Three huge explosions rocked the wall, sending plumes of flame into the air that were seen hundreds of miles away."

I held my breath, hoping against hope that somehow the grinders had succeeded. Feeble hopes that were quickly dashed.

"Melming Executive Director General Kirk Thatcher says some casualties were sustained, but the defenses held.

"'We suspected an attack was imminent. We were ready. Our troops fought bravely and successfully. A man thought to have masterminded the attack was captured in the fight.'"

"Beca?" I wondered out loud. This was more bad news.

"'He is being held for questioning.'"

"Torture, you mean," Fatima said bitterly.

"'We believe he has information that can lead us to the very top, to help us end this terror once and for all. To that end, more extraordinary rights have been granted to Melming Mining by the Global Governmental Council. These grinders have no rules. We must fight on their terms. We will be ruthless in rooting them out like the cancer they are.'

"The attack follows a series of smaller incidents,

including the sabotage of an abandoned mining rig in the Skagerrak strait and a guerilla attack on a medical helicopter that left a dozen people dead."

"Ha!" Elena laughed so loud they could probably hear it on the surface.

"Thatcher went on to say that some of the rebels escaped into the ground using stolen diggers. The country is on high alert for more attacks.

"Anyone with information is . . ."

I clicked off the radio. "Thatcher knows we weren't at HQ . . ."

"Or he'll coerce that from Beca, or whoever he's captured," Elena said.

"Which means he'll start looking for us somewhere else," Fatima finished.

Elena fired up the digger and we sped forward. We were less than an hour away from our destination. Was that enough time to find Melming and get him to believe us?

"Why did the grinders attack at all?" I wondered.

"They must have known the Oracle was gone. Thatcher made everyone aware he was at Melming HQ. Maybe it was as simple as revenge," Fatima suggested.

"Or it was a diversion," Elena said. "To help buy us some more time."

"Maybe," I said. "Beca guessed we weren't going to HQ?"

"Or he thought we were and was going there to help," Fatima said.

"Whatever the reason, it's grabbed Thatcher's attention for now. We can't waste that opportunity."

The minutes passed more quickly than I expected, the tension soon giving way to resignation, acceptance, and impatience. We were going to surface as close to the coordinates as possible—our recent dip in the channel warned us against risking one in the lake—and then continue on foot.

The rock flew past us and then we rose, cutting finally through mud and moss.

"We're here," Elena said. We emerged in the middle of a wood. Thick fog obscured almost everything, the clamminess of the air adding an otherworldliness to the scene.

We opened the cockpit lid slowly and could hear the sound of lapping waves not far away.

"Close call," Elena said.

"Let's get some camouflage for the digger," I said.

Fatima and I climbed out and began gathering as many dead branches and leaves as we could. Elena lowered the digger back into the ground, and in a few seconds climbed back out of the hole with our remaining blasters and one oxygen mask.

"The others are all empty," she said. She handed it to Fatima.

"Mandeep's," Fatima whispered. She clipped it to her belt and slung the blaster over her shoulder.

"And Chris. This was in the glove compartment. I thought you'd want it, here at the end."

She handed me Darcy's card. The dip in the water had almost ruined it. The images were smudged, the paper barely more than pulp. But I nodded, too choked up to say thanks, and put the paper in my pocket.

"So, Fearless, where to?"

I pointed west. "The Oracle said the sun was shining into Melming's room, off the lake, and it was morning. So that means the sun was in the east, hitting the water and the room. We need to head that way."

We covered the hole with the branches. It wasn't perfect cover, but it would keep anyone from seeing it from the sky.

We began marching silently through the trees and fog, toward the only person who could save us.

At least, that was my hope.

If I was wrong, we were marching to our doom.

Chapter Forty

Marching

The mist seemed to grow thicker as we hiked through a seemingly endless forest of scraggly pine trees and thick brush.

"I'm tempted to just blast a trail," Elena said, holding up her weapon.

"Just keep the sound of the water to our right and we'll follow the shoreline until we hit the cabin. Or whatever it is."

"And keep an eye out for a security perimeter," Elena said, looking down.

"Wires, cameras. The fog is helping at least," Fatima said. She stepped on a twig, snapping it in half. The sound was quickly swallowed up by the thick air.

"Hides a lot," Elena said. "And remember to trust no one. We have no idea if Melming is our friend or a friend of Thatcher's."

I let that thought disappear into the haze.

We continued on, the only sounds our breathing and the shuffle of pine needles. Occasionally a bird would fly overhead and we would pause.

Then the trees gave way to a clearing, and the cabin was right there in front of us as if it had materialized out of thin air. It seemed so small, humble. I had expected a huge compound, some kind of rich person's cottage, with tall walls and huge sweeping rooms.

This looked like the kind of place you might rent at a budget campsite. The outside was covered in wooden shingles, mostly gray with age. The roof was thick with moss. A stone walkway led down to a rocky beach. A small fishing boat lay upside down on a tuft of grass and dried seaweed.

"This is it?" Elena asked.

"Maybe it's the gardener's cottage?" I said.

"Or this is someone else's?" Fatima asked. But there didn't seem to be anything else nearby other than the gloomy silhouettes of tall trees.

Then we saw him. A bent figure shuffling around a small garden near the front walk. He was leaning over, picking up something from a patch of green near the front door. I watched him for a few seconds before he straightened uneasily and walked back inside.

"Melming," I said. I was about to call out to him when Elena put her hand over my mouth. She shook her head.

"How do we know he's alone?" she whispered.

She was right. I was so excited to be here, to see him alive, that I'd almost given our location away.

Melming walked into the cottage and the screen door closed with a bang, then clapped against the frame again before resting silently on its hinges.

"I didn't even hear a lock," I said.

"Doesn't mean there isn't one," Elena warned. "Let's split up. ANYTHING moves outside, you shoot it."

Elena walked around the back of the building. Fatima went toward the beach, her blaster raised and her eyes scanning the ground before each step.

I took a deep breath and made my way toward the front door.

I had to pass by the windows. I tried to lower myself so that I couldn't be seen, but my curiosity forced me to sneak a peek. The room was just the way the Oracle had described it. Wood-paneled walls. A huge oak desk. Melming was sitting in a leather chair, ripping up green leaves, then dropping the pieces into a steaming mug.

There were no screens on the window and I could smell herbs or flowers mixed with tea. My mouth watered.

"I see you, you know," he said, without looking up.

I froze.

"You by the garden. Why don't you come in and have a cup of tea with an old man? Or perhaps you are here to rob me?"

I couldn't speak. His voice, so familiar yet so strange, made me feel like this wasn't happening. This was all a dream.

"Or perhaps you have been robbed. What is that old saying? 'The cat has stolen my voice'? Something like that." He sighed and took a sip from his cup. "As you can see, this is just a humble cottage. I have little, but what I have is yours. Come in."

He looked straight at me, and then he froze. His mouth formed a shocked *O*. "No. It can't be!" he said. He dropped the mug, and it shattered on the floor. He began frantically searching for something on his desk.

A loud clicking rang out as metal panels began to lower over the windows.

The sound shook me out of my stupor. I ran to the door just as a panel was beginning to descend behind the screen.

I got on my belly and slid under feet-first right before

it slammed shut behind me, narrowly missing crushing my head.

I stood up, brushing dried pine needles off my legs.

Red lights lit up a path along the hallway floor. A brighter light shone from a doorway ahead and to my left. I held up my blaster and walked forward slowly, my back against the wall.

Melming was shuffling more papers in the den. Something heavy fell to the floor with a loud thump.

Melming shouted, "You're dead. You're dead."

There was more shuffling. I inched forward.

"Dead," he repeated. "Thatcher said you were all . . ." His voice trailed off. Hearing him use Thatcher's name sent a chill up my spine. Elena's voice echoed in my ears . . . *Trust no one.*

I reached the door and swung around, blaster raised.

Melming was sitting at his desk, slumped down. His arms lay limply across the arms of his chair. He wasn't holding any weapons.

He raised his eyes. "Make it quick." He nodded toward the blaster, then leaned forward, placing his hands on the desktop.

I lowered my weapon a few inches. "Mr. Melming. Sir," I said. "I'm not here to kill you. I'm here because we need your help."

"Help?" He considered the word and said again, "Help."

His eyes watered. He slumped more, looking less like the great scientist I'd remembered, or imagined, and more like my grandfather before he'd died. Sad. Tired. Confused.

I stepped forward, taking in as much of the room as I could. The blast screens had completely shut out any outside light. Elena and Fatima were probably trying to find a way in—by stealth or by shooting. The lack of any sound showed just how thick and impenetrable the barrier was. But we were alone, at least. Melming's voice jerked my eyes forward again.

"Thatcher told me you had survived the first grinder attacks."

Melming knew we hadn't been killed? My legs felt weak.

"Then he told me you had turned. Captured by grinder rebels. Tortured until you became one of them," Melming said quietly, more to himself than to me. "But he said . . . he said that he had taken care of the Perses rebellion."

Taken care of us.

"He tried," I said. "But you need to know that I am not a rebel."

Melming's head snapped up. "Then show me your arm."

I let out a deep sigh as I rolled up the sleeve of my uniform, revealing the *M* tattoo.

Melming nodded almost sadly. "Just as Thatcher told me."

"I'm proud of this mark," I said. "But it's not what Thatcher says it is. It's a mark of friendship. Of solidarity with the kids who survived. And the ones who didn't. But we are not rebels, sir. *We* were attacked. By Thatcher. By his men. And we came here to Earth to end this."

Melming lifted his left hand, revealing a glowing red button on his desk console. "You can tell him that yourself," Melming said. "He'll be here in just a few minutes."

Chapter Forty-One

Trapped

My mind raced. Thatcher knew we were here. He was coming to get us. Melming had told him to come get us. He'd betrayed us. My first thought wasn't about me but Elena and Fatima, trapped outside with no idea Thatcher was on his way. They were sitting ducks.

I held the blaster up higher. "Tell him to stop. Tell him it was a false alarm."

Melming stared at the end of the blaster. "So you *are* here to shoot me," he said. "Go ahead. As I said. I am an old man now. I have lived my life."

My finger twitched close to the trigger as I fought back a mix of anger, shock, and sadness. But I closed my eyes and lowered the weapon. "No. I told you, I'm not here to kill you. I am not a killer. But you and Thatcher have been working together? I can't believe it."

Melming seemed confused again. "Of course we work together," he said.

"Why?"

"He believes in the mission just as much as I do. Just as much as my granddaughter . . . did." His voice sounded weak.

His granddaughter. The Oracle. It was my only chance, but it depended on everything I had believed in, or still did, being right.

I rushed to the edge of his desk and leaned in close. "Your granddaughter did believe in the Great Mission. I did. I still do. Thatcher betrayed you. He's been lying to you."

Melming shook his head. "No. She . . . she helped the grinders. The grinders I sent into the mines. She helped them destroy everything." He pressed his eyes closed, pinching the space between them with his fingers. His hands trembled. The Oracle had said Melming approved of using grinders but had never reconciled himself to it. He was clearly wrestling with something deep inside now. Shame, maybe? Guilt?

"I knew your granddaughter," I said.

He opened his eyes, the brilliant blue of them locked

onto mine. "She was a traitor," he said.

Everything began to spill out as fast as a waterfall. "No. No, she wasn't. You have to believe me. She suspected Thatcher wasn't what he said he was, didn't believe what he said he believed. She knew he was using the Great Mission as a front to take control of Melming Mining, of everything. She knew he was lying to you. He still is. She tried to help us. She died telling us that we needed to find you. That only you could help us. I . . ."

He narrowed his eyes. "When did you see her die?"

"Two days ago. Along with my friend Mandeep. Thatcher killed them in a cavern deep underground. She told us to find you. Then he crushed them."

Melming shook his head. "You're lying. She was killed in a shuttle crash. She was trying to escape and the shuttle blew up. I saw it happen. I saw her get on the shuttle. I saw it explode."

I had no idea what he was talking about. The Oracle had never mentioned anything like that to me.

"No. I saw her. Spoke to her."

"Bah. Whoever you saw was not my granddaughter." His sadness was now giving way to anger.

Thatcher would be here any minute. Time was running out.

I looked around again at the paneled walls. The desk. The open door to the nearby kitchen. Thatcher might walk through that doorway any second. I could even see the radio the Oracle had mentioned. Mentioned . . .

"She told me a story," I said suddenly. "She told me a story about the day you announced the Great Mission."

Melming turned his head to look at a point between his feet. I continued, recalling every detail.

"She told me about the light from the lake. It was morning. Breakfast was in the kitchen."

His eyes seemed to scan the room, moving from location to location as I went on.

"And she told me how she sat at your feet and watched you press a secret button under the desk that allowed you to tap in to all the satellites in space. She told me how you made sure everyone, everywhere, heard what you had to say."

He turned back to me and stopped. "Impossible."

"I know about the Interface," I said. "She was your granddaughter. She was my friend. She died telling me this story. She knew you and she were the only two people in the world who knew about that button. She said you talked about it later, over toast and marmalade. How you made her tea with ginger."

Tears welled up in his eyes. His lips quivered.

"She was my wonderful genius," he said. "I knew I could show her. Even at that young age, I knew she would understand. Such a mind. Such an amazing mind." He wiped the tears from his cheek.

"Her name was Tatiana. But you called her Tuti."

He nodded. "Yes. Yes."

Now I realized why she had told me so many tiny details. Not just about the Interface but about everything else that day. That moment had been important to her and to Melming. If she'd been tortured for information, she might have revealed the big things but not the small ones that, maybe, meant even more to them both.

"Tell Thatcher to stand down."

He shook his head. "It's too late. He'd warned me I might be a target. I didn't care. But when I saw it was you . . . Christopher, I'm so sorry. He won't be fooled. He thought you might come for me." Melming pressed the red button again.

There was a loud click and the screens began to slowly rise, the metal strips clacking against each other as they began to recede into the walls. Sunlight crept in along the carpeted floor.

I fumbled inside my coat and pulled out one of the phones Beca had give me.

"It's not too late," I said, turning on the power. A

slow circle spun as it woke up. I was so close.

But we were interrupted by a burst of gunfire and shouts from the grounds outside. Blaster fire ripped into wood. Dirt flew against the windows, the sunbeams illuminating billows of dust.

Thatcher had arrived. Elena and Fatima were buying me time by ambushing him and his troops. They were going to die. I was going to die. But Melming could still help the grinders. At the very least, part of me just wanted him to know the truth. What, and who, had really destroyed his dreams of a Great Mission.

I placed the phone in front of him. "When it powers up, press play," I said. I rushed to the window with my blaster as the screens continued to rise.

I looked outside. Troops were pouring from the sky, rappelling down from a huge blue-black transport.

I couldn't see any sign of Elena or Fatima, but every few seconds a blast from a different location would hit the transport, or a soldier, or a tree trunk. The impact sending splinters flying like knives through the air.

Thatcher's troops weren't bothering to fire back. Not yet. They were just trying to get to the ground, where they started fanning out into the woods.

I raised my own blaster and rested it on the window-sill. I aimed up just as Thatcher himself, bent but still huge and menacing, made his way to the gangplank. I raised my sight and took aim. I pulled the trigger.

Nothing happened.

"Those weapons don't work in here," Melming said.

I stared down at the blaster. It seemed powered and ready. "What? How?"

"A chip inside deactivates the gun within these walls. I made sure the military put one in every weapon. Not that they knew what it was really for."

"You knew I couldn't kill you," I said, sliding down the wall to hide my head. The panels were now raised up entirely, the light streaming in.

Melming nodded. "It was a test. One of many you have passed today. I am sorry again . . . for everything that has happened. I was blind. A fool. An absolute fool."

His face was lit up slightly by the screen of the phone. It was on now. He was about to see just how foolish he had been to trust Thatcher. And how Thatcher had abused that trust to destroy Melming's own hopes.

I felt a sudden rush of sadness for him.

The shooting outside had stopped. I didn't dare look up. I knew what I'd see. Thatcher, triumphant, striding toward the cabin, ready to finish this. Expecting Melming to have kept me busy until he, Thatcher, could come and get rid of the remains of the "rebellion."

Melming must have touched the screen because I could hear, faintly, the sound of the doctor pleading for Nazeem's life. Followed by the sound of Thatcher ending it. The phone went silent just as the back door swung open, and the sound of heavy footsteps, with a slight limp, signaled the arrival of Thatcher.

Melming looked up from the phone and stared at me. Before he or I could say anything, Thatcher's voice boomed through the room.

"Hans. I see that this grinder rebel has tried to kill you. Good work capturing him."

Melming looked at Thatcher, then back to me. "Yes," he yelled. "He tried to shoot me. But his blaster doesn't seem to work."

I stared at Melming, confused. Why was he speaking so loudly? What was going on? Only then did I notice that Melming had moved one hand under his desk. The phone I'd given him was nowhere to be seen. Had he betrayed me after all?

Thatcher unclipped a blaster pistol from his belt and walked over toward me.

My execution was about to be broadcast all around the globe.

Chapter Forty-Two

Interface

Thatcher didn't shoot, but he grabbed me by the shoulder and said, softly so only I could hear, "Nichols, you insect. Did you honestly think this would work?" Then he turned to Melming and added in a louder voice, "I'll take this traitor back to headquarters for questioning. Our troops are even now rooting out the last few rebels from the surrounding woods. If he tries to escape, I'll shoot him."

He wasn't even looking at me. I took my useless blaster and smashed it against his knee. He flinched in pain but didn't let go. His face twisted in a crooked smile. "Resisting arrest? Excellent."

He threw me against the wall. Pain shot through my

arm as my shoulder gave an audible crack. I fell to the floor, screaming in agony.

Darcy's card somehow slipped out of my pocket and settled on the floor between us. Thatcher picked it up. He unfurled the decaying paper, flakes falling like snow to the floor, and laughed.

"You brought this all the way back from that godforsaken planet?" he smirked. "How incredibly pathetic."

He stood over me and ripped the card to shreds, letting the pieces fall on my chest. "And that's just what will happen to your little friend Darcy when my troops get back to Perses."

Furious, I quickly swung my legs, sending him sprawling.

He was up like a shot, his blaster aimed at my head.

"Any other ideas, you murderous grinder?" he said.

My arm throbbed.

"I wouldn't be the first child you've murdered," I yelled, struggling to find my feet. "There's a whole graveyard on Perses filled with them."

Thatcher placed a boot on my arm, sending more lightning bolts of pain through my body. He pushed me back to the floor and then smiled. I was confused. The Interface was activated. Why would he want that made public?

But he pointed at a small box on the chest of his own body armor. "I'll just edit that little bit out later," he smiled. "Yes. Setting up the stage and then making a little movie. An idea I got from an old friend of yours."

"Friend?" I asked. Was he talking about Melming?

Thatcher stepped aside and one of his soldiers walked forward, holding Pavel by the shoulders. Pavel's face was swollen and cut, his left eye swollen shut.

I gasped.

Pavel glared at me with nothing but hate. He spat on my cheek as Thatcher shoved him to the floor next to me.

Thatcher knelt down, his shadow covering my face. "Your buddy here is a suicide bomber," he whispered. Thatcher reached over and lifted the collar of Pavel's shirt, exposing a crude vest packed with bricks of explosives.

"Tsk, tsk, tsk. It will certainly be horrible when that goes off, destroying everything here and you along with it. But it will be more evidence of grinder treachery." He pulled up Pavel's shirtsleeve, revealing a fresh double-M tattoo. Then he slapped him across the face.

"All the pieces are in place," Thatcher said, standing up, "for a grand finale. Pavel very helpfully suggested you would try to reach out to your hero Melming. We've had a task force stationed not far away for days in case you showed up. Hans signaled me the second you arrived. Trusting your 'friends.' Weakness. That's why I'm about to win."

Pavel groaned next to me. His arms, I realized, were tied to his sides. He couldn't disarm the bomb if he'd wanted to.

Thatcher was going to make it look like Pavel and I were in this together, attacking Melming and then dying in the blast. Or that I was a hostage. Whatever story he'd decided on, he'd have it all packaged perfectly for public consumption.

But Melming was also broadcasting everything. Why? I knew he was pushing the button that activated the Interface and took over the global communications network. Anyone with any device, including everyone from people at home to government leaders in the halls of power, would see what was happening. Live. What was going on?

Then it hit me. Melming and Tatiana were the only people who knew about the Interface. Thatcher didn't know he was being watched. He didn't realize what was happening. But Melming did. And Melming knew that I did too. This was the trial, the trial I'd wanted from the beginning. I almost had to suppress an urge to laugh.

I had been marshaling my arguments for months. Now it was time to strike, not with weapons but with words, before I died.

"I realize what I hate most about you," I said, as loudly and clearly as I could.

"What?" Thatcher said, kicking me in the arm with his boot.

I winced but fought the pain. "That you think you get to decide who's human and who's not. Who deserves to live and who doesn't."

Thatcher sneered and raised his gun. "Everyone thinks they get to do that. Everyone decides who is good and who's bad. I just do something about it. And I'm going to do something about you right now. After all, you and this other grinder rebel," he pointed at Pavel, "just broke in here to kill the leader of the Great Mission."

"You killed your own troops on Perses rather than let anyone know you'd murdered an injured child. A grinder. A friend of mine."

Thatcher stole a furtive glance at the guards near the door. "That's a lie and you know it," he said. "It was your grinder friend who shot the guard. I made sure he paid for that."

"And the doctor?"

"What doctor? There was no doctor there."

"She was there. She told you Nazeem needed help and you killed her."

"Lies. If you check the records of our mission to Perses, you will see no mention of any doctor."

I realized he'd simply wiped the record clean. I gritted my teeth. I needed to keep him talking.

"You killed Nazeem. In cold blood. A child."

"He shot at us. I shot back. I didn't check his birth certificate."

"There's a video," I said.

Now Thatcher beamed. "Is there? Because the only copy I know of was destroyed along with a digger we found in the woods outside this very cabin not more than thirty minutes ago. Your 'friend' very helpfully told me about that too." He smiled at Pavel, who turned his head away.

So the digger had been found and destroyed. Now it was my turn to flinch. What did that mean for Elena and Fatima?

"And before you tell me about the copies of the video that your late friend—Beca, was it?—was supposed to send around, let me enlighten you. He very helpfully told us where to find the stash. Of course, a few phones might be out there, but it's old technology and not a lot of people know how to use it. We can easily find and destroy any we missed before they spread too far."

"So what do you plan to do with me and Pavel?" I said.

"A suicide bomber and an assassin?" Thatcher said. "What would you expect me to do? Wait a minute . . ." He paused, thinking. "No. I have a better idea." He pulled a pair of handcuffs, very old and rusty, from a pouch in his pants and leaned down, clasping them around my wrists. "Better," he said. "Instead of an assassin, we have a hostage! Christopher Nichols. Captured on Perses and brought to Earth. Killed along with the traitor, Pavel. How sad."

He stood back up and pointed at his camera. "Showtime."

Thatcher turned around to face the guards. "Tell me if they do anything suspicious." The guards nodded.

I didn't move. I knew I would die, but I didn't care anymore. People would finally see what Thatcher was. Who he was. Evil.

"Grinders have just as much right to live as anyone else," I yelled.

Thatcher continued to face the guards but called back over his shoulder. "Oh, I know that. And you know that. But those idiots out there"—he jerked his head toward the window—"they need somebody to blame for all their troubles. A bunch of poor grunts who work underground? No great loss."

I had to work to keep my composure. Everything he said made me sick, but I had to keep him talking. It was all more and more evidence. I looked over at Melming, his hand still under the desk, his gaze lowered. He was keeping quiet but was listening intently. I noticed his other hand was clenched in a fist. It must have been torture for him to hear the truth.

"And just imagine how much more people will hate them when they realize the grinders killed their hostage, a boy they kidnapped on Perses."

I closed my eyes. I had seen so many people die.

I could hear Thatcher breathing, making sure his shot would hit me once and be fatal. He added in a whisper only I could hear, "And blew up the founder of the Great Mission as well."

I needed to act. Now.

"This is who he is," I yelled.

Thatcher stopped. "What did you say?"

"This is who he is," I yelled even louder. "He's a killer. He wants power and nothing else, and he's risked the whole world to help himself. He attacked us on Perses. He's the one who kills children!"

Thatcher looked around the room. "Who are you talking to?"

His eyes stopped on Melming. Melming was holding a blaster of his own, his other hand still under the desk.

"I'm afraid he's been talking to everyone," Melming said.

Thatcher eyes narrowed. "What the hell are you talking about, old man? We disabled your network access ages ago." He began to falter, his legs wobbly.

Melming shook his head. "My granddaughter was smarter than you can ever imagine. I didn't share all my secrets with you or anyone else. I worried she had. But then this young man told me a story."

"A story? You are a senile old man who has lost his mind."

There was a loud whooshing sound from the woods and the renewed blasts of gunfire. A huge ship was landing outside.

"Not everyone is loyal to you," Melming said. Then he held up the phone I'd handed him. "I've also fed the raw data from this phone onto the server. Some of us are old enough to remember how to use these. The video is now being broadcast around the world, along with the pathetic look on your face."

Thatcher looked from me to Melming and back again.

"It's over," I said. "You lose."

Thatcher shook with rage. He sputtered, his eyes darting about like a trapped animal. He stared at his blaster and smirked. "I knew there was a reason you wanted those chips in these," he said. "Luckily I had mine taken out."

Before anyone could react, he raised his blaster at Melming and fired. The shot hit Melming in the shoulder, and he flew back against the wall before falling to the floor behind his desk. Blood stained the wood.

"NO!" I yelled.

Pavel stayed motionless but began to cry. "I don't want to die."

I struggled to get up but had only made it to my knees when Thatcher trained the gun on me, his face twisted with fury, his hand trembling. I could see his mind racing for a solution, some way out.

"There is no way out this time," I said calmly. "Fire."

"No one is watching now." Thatcher locked his eyes on mine. "I should have killed you when I had the chance."

Before he could squeeze the trigger, there was an enormous crash. The ceiling caved in between us as the remains of the troop carrier smashed through the timbers. A cloud of dust and smoke filled the room.

"Move!" I said to Pavel. We rolled to our left, finding cover behind a giant chunk of plaster and twisted metal. I struggled to tear my hands free. Pavel did the same.

Thatcher coughed, waving both hands in the air. He'd lost his gun in the crash.

"NICHOLS!" he yelled, kicking aside debris and tossing it around the room. "I'm going to wring your neck!"

A helicopter began to descend on the lawn outside, the wind from its rotors sucking the dust through the now-shattered windows.

In seconds, we'd be visible again.

More explosions and blaster fire split the air outside.

One of the guards yelled in, "Sir, we need to go now."

The air cleared. I ducked as low as I could behind the debris. Thatcher scanned the room for any sign of us. He turned to the guards. "Start shooting a path to the copter. I'll be there in a second." He pulled a small box from his pack. "There's more than one way to kill a traitor," he said.

"The detonator," Pavel said beside me. "If we can reach it before he . . ." I stood to run at Thatcher, to try to save us.

But Thatcher pushed a button and the box began to beep. He tossed it on a pile of rubble across the floor from me. "Goodbye, Nichols," Thatcher said. "There are still people who will believe me when I tell them grinders were behind all this. Too bad you won't be around to see me rise again."

He turned to go, then stopped.

The guards were standing in the doorway, arms raised. They took a step backward.

Thatcher didn't hesitate. He ran up to one of them and wrapped his arm around his neck, using him as a shield. The man gagged and fought in vain to release Thatcher's grip. "You let me go, or this man dies." They backed across the floor.

"I don't care about him, or you," said a familiar voice. My heart leapt. Elena!

She limped into the den. Her clothes were scorched and covered in blood. Her face was burned and scarred. She held her blaster high. But I knew the blaster wouldn't work. The chip would shut it down. The guards didn't know that yet, obviously, or they would have fought back.

"Elena, don't shoot. Melming helped. He believed us. The whole world knows. They know what happened." I tried to make eye contact with her, to somehow warn her that she was in incredible danger without alerting the guards. But she kept her eyes trained on Thatcher, her blaster aimed right at his head.

"Elena. It's over! GO!"

"Roger that, Fearless Leader." Elena nodded but marched forward silently, the blaster pointed at Thatcher. She waved at the other guard, who dropped his weapon and crept out the door before breaking into a sprint.

"Rat from a sinking spaceship," Elena said.

Thatcher tightened his grip on the other guard's neck and stepped forward. "I'm going through you and then out that door," he said. Why didn't he fight? Was he still weak?

She shook her head.

"You let me go," Thatcher said. "Or we are all going to die when the bomb strapped to your friend Pavel explodes."

"Fine," Elena said. "We all die. But you are going to go first."

Thatcher released the guard, who fell to the floor, hacking.

I realized too late that Thatcher had spied his blaster in the rubble and had been quietly inching toward it. He stood still, defiant. "Go ahead," he said, smirking.

"Elena, NO!" I said. She pulled the trigger but nothing happened. Her eyes opened wide as she stared at the barrel in shock.

In one quick motion, Thatcher reached down, grabbed his weapon, and fired.

Chapter Forty-Three
The End

Time stopped.

Thatcher teetered on his feet, like a tree that's been cut but hasn't fallen. A crimson stain spread across his back. He stared at his chest, incredulous.

Then he fell.

His bulk sent a spiral through the smoke as he crashed to the floor with a loud thud. The guard ran for the door. He pushed past Elena. She smacked into the doorframe, then slid down to her knees. Her right shoulder was smoldering and the side of her face was burned. She began to fall over. I ran to her, tripping on the rubble, and caught her in my arms.

The weight of her on my injured shoulder was

excruciating, but I struggled to hold her as still as possible.

She looked up, but I could tell she could barely see me. Her right eye was closed, the skin around it burned. She struggled to breathe. "Elena, it's me. Christopher. You're going to be okay. But you have to stay with me. Okay?"

She nodded, ever so slightly. I tried to think about what Mandeep would do. Elena's wounds weren't bleeding, but they were deep. She was in shock. *Keep her alert. Keep her mind racing. Get help.* Okay. I could do that.

"Now. I'm going to lay you down and get some help, okay?"

She nodded.

"Good. Good. I'll keep talking to you."

I laid her down on the carpet. "Okay, I'm going to see if anyone can help."

I turned to take in the den. I tried to describe everything I could see, just to keep Elena focused on the here and now.

"It's still smoking, but I see Melming. He's . . . he's dead."

Melming lay on his desk, his eyes lifeless, his fingers wrapped around the handle of his blaster. It was still smoking from where he'd shot Thatcher. It had been his dying act. If I could get Elena medical attention, it might just have saved her life.

"Christopher," said a voice from the floor.

Pavel sat cross-legged, the detonator in his right hand. It continued to blink, now even faster.

"Pavel," I said. "We need to go."

He shook his head. "*You* need to go. There's only a minute left on the timer. I tried to dismantle it. I can't even get the these stupid explosives off." He was crying, pawing at the deadly jacket.

The shooting outside had stopped. The guard must have told the troops Thatcher was dead. There was no option left but to surrender. I could hear shouting and yelling, but it was the noise of troops barking orders, not the screams of battle.

I put Elena down and scurried over to Pavel. I did my best to loosen the straps on the jacket, but the detonator continued to blink and the straps refused to budge.

"Pavel." I choked back tears. "Your mom was a hero, a genius. Like you."

"Mom . . ." he said, staring straight ahead. "I miss her . . ."

"She worked with the grinders. She helped build the beacon."

He nodded slowly. But then he looked at me, his eyes flashing. "She was no grinder," he spat.

"Pavel. Despite everything, you were one of us . . .

I'm so sorry I left you behind. I . . ."

"GET OUT NOW!" He kicked out, sending me falling backward. Then he shuffled back toward the desk, still trying to wrestle off the jacket.

Elena moaned in pain and I hurried back to her. There was no way she would be able to stand. I was going to have to lift her, and I wasn't sure I could do it. But I knew I had to. I had to.

I knelt down and slipped my handcuffed hands under her back. I bit my lip as I stood up, but the sting took away some of the shooting pain in my shoulder.

I screamed, but I held her as steady as possible as I hurried away. The scream seemed to stir Elena. "Chris. Is he . . ."

"Yes," I said, grimacing. "It's over."

She gave a weak smile and went limp in my arms.

I ran as fast as I could, each step making me weaker. There were voices ahead, and I focused on them to keep me going.

I smashed right into the door of the cabin, righted myself, and stumbled out just as the bomb exploded. I felt a rush of flame on my back, tasted the burn of blasted wood, and fell to my knees.

A blurry figure ran at me through the smoke, and everything began to spin.

Chapter Forty-Four

Landing

I woke up to music. Light, beautiful, slow music. It sounded familiar, but I couldn't place it. The ringing in my ears didn't help.

I opened my eyes. A woman I'd never seen before was standing over me. She was wearing a deep-blue suit. She wasn't a doctor or a nurse, as far as I could tell. An ID badge hung from her lapel.

I noticed with a start it was a badge for Melming Mining. I tried to sit up in my bed, pushing with my feet. "Go away," I said. "Get out!" But straps held me in place and my shoulder screamed in protest.

The woman held up both hands in a sign of surrender and spoke.

"Christopher Nichols. I know how hard this past year has been. I know what you have gone through, and you are right to mistrust this uniform, and this company, and this mission."

I tensed. No one in a uniform had done anything but lie to me and try to kill me. But she kept her hands still, a sad smile breaking across her lips.

"Who are you?" My voice sounded strained, weak, barely a whisper. My throat burned.

She lowered her hands. "My name is Alenia Maxwell. I was a friend of the one you called the Oracle, Tatiana. I worked with her to try to expose Thatcher."

"You stayed on the inside?" I asked, my suspicion on full red-alert.

"Yes. Until recently." She took a few deep breaths. "I was feeding her as much information as I could. Thatcher's people discovered me. The past few months I spent in prison."

She held up her hands again and turned them around. They were covered in scars. "I have also been interrogated."

I nodded. And relaxed. A little. I looked around the room. The last time I'd been in an actual hospital room, on Perses, I'd been surrounded by propaganda posters telling me how amazing the Great Mission was going to be. Telling me how I needed to play my obedient little part to make it a success.

The walls here were blank.

Alenia Maxwell dropped her hands to her sides. "But we could never have achieved what you did. We thank you. We have begun purging the corporation of Thatcher's . . ."

"Where are my friends?" I said, cutting her off. Nothing else mattered.

Alenia looked at me and smiled. "You'll see them soon."

Them. She'd said *them*.

"And we've made arrangements for a new exploration party to travel to Perses."

My pulse raced.

She nodded. "We have been in contact, briefly, with Therese and Darcy. They are fine, but the weather there has become very unpredictable. We feel it is best that they return to Earth."

I cried for a full minute, the sobs sending stabs of pain through my body. But I couldn't help it. They were alive. They were alive.

Unable to reach my own face, I lay there, the tears pouring down my cheeks, wetting my pillow. Alenia waited, head down, until I stopped, then reached over and dabbed my face dry. I could feel my grip on consciousness begin to slip away. But I had more questions.

"How about . . ." My voice cracked and trailed off.

Alenia misunderstood. "The grinders? They have been offered absolution and amnesty. And a vow that there will no longer be children in mines. Or branding of people as less than full citizens, or full humans."

I struggled to ask about Elena, Fatima . . . but my voice stubbornly refused to return.

"I am sorry for everything this uniform represents," she said. "But it is not good to dwell on the past. The world is still the same world. The problems are still the same problems. We can't solve them all in one blow. But we can make sure that the solutions Thatcher put forward . . . they won't be supported again."

I strained to lift my head, to plead with my eyes for more news, but the effort drained what energy I had left and I fell back.

Alenia smiled and straightened my sheets. "Things will get better. You will too. You all will."

A nurse came into view. "Time for your medicine," she said. And without hesitation, she stabbed me in the arm with a needle. Within seconds I was fast asleep.

I don't know how long I slept for, but when I woke up again Alenia Maxwell was gone. The restraints were off, but my body still felt like it had crash-landed. I was in a different room. This one had posters, but not for Melming Mining. These had images of flowers and kittens, and a dog with a stethoscope. "Listen to your dog-tor," it read.

It was so silly, so amazingly kitschy, that I laughed, then winced in pain, then laughed again.

"Well, someone is feeling better!"

I looked to my left. Fatima was sitting up in a hospital bed, reading a book.

I was too shocked, too happy, to speak.

"Nice to have you back, Fearless." She gave a wave.

I choked up but found my voice. "Not coming to hug me?"

Fatima flipped off her bedsheet to reveal a stump where her right leg used to be.

"Oh, Fatima. I'm so sorry," I muttered.

"It's okay. Got this back at the battle at Melming's cabin when I tried to jump in the digger. Could have been a lot worse. The new prosthetic they gave me isn't bad. I'm just not that used to it yet."

I gazed around the room. There was one more bed. But it was empty. The sheets unruffled. My heart sank. Footsteps from the hallway jolted me back, but it was a nurse who walked into the room. "I'm here for Fatima's morning walk. You're welcome to join us." He helped Fatima climb out of bed and into a wheelchair.

I shook my head.

"Fatima. Is Elena . . ." I stopped myself, too afraid of the answer she might give.

But she looked at me and winked.

"Like I've said before, that girl is a force of nature. Be *patient*. Get it?" Then she laughed and gave me a wave as she and the nurse left the room.

Moments later there was more shuffling from the hallway. I sat up, my shoulder aching, as Elena limped into the room.

She had a patch over her right eye, and her right arm and leg were in casts. I had never seen a more wonderful sight. She saw me and smiled the biggest smile possible, then her face twisted in pain.

"That hurts," she said. "No more smiling."

"I can't help it," I said.

She made her way over and smacked me on the arm.

"Fearless Leader? More like Drowsy Leader," she laughed. We just stared dumbly at each other for what seemed like an hour, amazed to be together after everything.

"Well, we make a pretty picture, don't we?" I said at last.

"Well earned," Elena said, slapping her cast. "Think of these as souvenirs. Mementos of momentous events. Battle scars for battle stars."

"You've clearly been working on those," I said.

"Don't sleep in so late next time," Elena said. She sat down on the edge of my bed. More silence. I just kept staring at her. There was almost too much to say.

"I talked to Darcy," she said at last, breaking the ice. "They hooked up a link to some transmitter they found in the abandoned core-scraper."

I looked away. "How is she?"

"She's good. Taller. Therese took really good care of both of them. Darcy seemed even a little excited at the idea of coming home."

"Did she say anything about me?"

Elena gave a deep sigh. "It's tough for her, you know? She'll come around. I did tell her you might be willing to get her a puppy once she comes back."

"A puppy? Seriously?"

Elena smiled. "Sometimes you have to think like a little kid. She seemed to actually soften a bit at the idea. If I were you, I'd start puppy shopping."

I smiled back. "Only if you come along."

Elena reached over and took my left hand. She interlaced her fingers with what were left of mine. I took my other hand and ran it through her hair, gently touching the bandages.

"Who needs two eyes," she said. "It only takes one to aim."

"I'm so sorry," I said.

"Sorry for what?"

"For not saving everyone. For not being a better leader."

"You did your best. We all did."

She gave my hand a squeeze.

The music began playing again. The same song I'd heard when I woke up the first time. It was also the same song I'd heard at the Blackout Bash when Elena and I had slow danced. Right before the bombs fell.

"'Venus' from Holst's *The Planets*."

Elena nodded. "'The Bringer of Peace.'" It was coming from a speaker by her bed.

"That's yours?"

"Yeah. I always liked that song."

"You're kidding, right?"

"I never told you this, but that song was my request." Elena squeezed my hand. "Someone stole it from me. I'm taking it back."

"On your own?"

"It's not that kind of song."

"You need a best friend to help out?" I said.

"Maybe someone more than that. It's going to take a lot more than Armageddon to keep me from hanging out with you, Christopher Nichols."

We sat together for a while, listening and holding hands.

"Hey, maybe we can go out for real tomorrow."

"A dance party?"

"Our last dance was rudely interrupted," I joked.

Elena leaned close to me, her breath on my cheek warm and sweet. "You do know what happens at midnight on New Year's Eve, right, Chris?"

I smiled. "Yeah. People wear goofy party hats."

She leaned over and kissed me, softly.

And the Earth, finally, seemed a better place.

Acknowledgments

First of all, a thanks to the types of people who read dedications.

I always try to make this bit of the book a little different, and thanks for paying attention to the details.

To be one hundred percent honest, I never thought this book would happen. You can check out the old posts on my blog if you want the full story, but the bottom line is that I owe a gigantic THANKS to you—the readers who fought to have this book written and published.

You helped spread the word about MiNRs, and that, in the end, is the only way a story can spread. Fighting for what you believe in is never easy. It can drain you. It can demoralize you. But you did it, which means the world to me. And maybe more so for MiNRs than it would for any of my other books.

MiNRs is many things, but above all it's a story of fighting, even when we don't want to. But we always need to fight for the things we believe in, the people we love. Or else someone else will fight to take them away . . . and we'll let them.

For Chris, Elena, and Fatima, that fight is with weapons. They don't choose this or want it, but they accept it.

It's a fight no child should ever face. But real children are forced to fight in our world today.

For the MiNRs, what separates them from others aren't the rules of their fight but the way they choose to face it. They choose love, family, and mercy over cruelty, violence, and hate. There's no fairy-book magic to this—they lose a lot along the way—but they don't sink to the level of Thatcher.

Not all fights are violent, or even battles in the traditional sense. In fact, for me, the toughest ones happen in your head and are fought with words and ideas.

There's an exchange in this book where the kids talk about scapegoating. Fatima argues it's worse than violence. And my editor (the awesome Patricia Ocampo on this book) and I had a back-and-forth about this.

Because, for me, the scapegoating is worse. It's

foundational to any violence that happens later. Attacking someone we see as the same as us? That's horrible! We recoil in shock.

But attacking someone who is different is way easier, and people will join in and support it because "*they* deserve it."

Try saying "we deserve it." Now try saying "they deserve it." Which is easier?

And it's so insidious. It doesn't actually begin with hate. It begins with searches for simple answers. The world is complicated, and that can be a really hard truth to recognize. And it makes it really hard to figure out what you need to do to make good choices.

So we pretend that isn't the way the world works. It's easier to see the world as simple.

It starts when we blame *them* for *their* problems. It's their fault they are poor, they don't work hard enough. It's their fault they are violent, because that's what *they* are like.

So much easier than saying, "Wow, the world is complicated, and some people are poor and violent for all sorts of reasons. Maybe the two are even related and poverty breeds the sorts of desperation that leads to some types of violence." And that's just the tip of the complexity iceberg, as they say.

And once you accept that simple worldview of *them vs. us*, the rest can devolve quickly.

They don't just cause their problems, they cause ours. *They* are opposed to what we stand for and are a threat to our way of life. This type of prejudice is what Thatcher exploits to turn people against grinders, and toward him.

But *they* are *you*.

We are we.

And above all, love is love. That's what breaks the cycle—loving others.

Loving them and not judging them.

It's easy to hold on to hate.

Pavel does.

Thatcher does.

But Chris doesn't.

Elena doesn't.

Fatima—a member of a "they"—doesn't.

And that makes all the difference.

Hate might win sometimes, but it makes the world a worse place.

Love might lose, but it still makes the world a better place.

It's tougher to actually promote love.

You need to fight to push yourself, and push others, to do just that.